STARS IN HER EYES

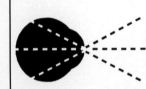

This Large Print Book carries the
Seal of Approval of N.A.V.H.

STARS IN HER EYES

ERICA VETSCH

THORNDIKE PRESS

A part of Gale, Cengage Learning

GALE
CENGAGE Learning·

Detroit • New York • San Francisco • New Haven, Conn • Waterville, Maine • London

GALE
CENGAGE Learning

LIBRARY OF CONGRESS CATALOGING-IN-PUBLICATION DATA

Vetsch, Erica.
    Stars in her eyes / by Erica Vetsch. — Large print ed.
      p. cm. — (Thorndike Press large print Christian fiction)
    ISBN-13: 978-1-4104-5196-5 (hardcover)
    ISBN-10: 1-4104-5196-8 (hardcover)
    1. Man-woman relationships—Fiction. 2. Actresses—Fiction. 3. Clergy—Fiction. 4. Large type books. I. Title.
PS3622.E886S73 2012
813'.6—dc23   2012022624

Published in 2012 by arrangement with Barbour Publishing, Inc.

Printed in Mexico
1 2 3 4 5 6 7 16 15 14 13 12

For Katie Ganshert.
We need another field trip to Galena.

ONE

Martin City, Colorado, Early Spring, 1886
Pastor Silas Hamilton had become adept at dodging matrimony-minded maidens and their matchmaking mamas, but he'd never encountered a mother as determined as Mrs. Drabble.

Beatrice Drabble had proven resourceful in finding ways to throw her daughter Alicia into his path, and he'd nearly exhausted all valid excuses. Not that he was against marriage, and Alicia Drabble was nice enough. But she wasn't the girl for him.

"I do hope you'll accept our luncheon invitation *this* time." Mrs. Drabble tilted her head back to peer up at him from under the feather-adorned awning she called a hat. Her button-black eyes bored into him like a rock drill. "You've been previously engaged for three weeks straight. Alicia has been so disappointed. She does enjoy your company. And we have a new set of pictures for the stereopticon. Natives from Africa. I thought you'd be interested, since you've been encouraging your parishioners to support African missions. . . ." She left the statement hanging, arching her dark eyebrows at him and drawing her lips into their habitual pucker.

He swallowed, his insides squirming. Invitations made under the guise of church work were always the most difficult to evade.

Conversations buzzed around them as people filed out of their pews and stood in line to shake his hand before heading home to a hot meal and a quiet afternoon. Spring sunshine streamed through the brand-new, stained glass windows that marched down the sides of the church, throwing blocks of color on his congregation as they milled and chatted. The installation of those windows — special ordered all the way from Germany — marked the end of the first major tussle he'd encountered in this, his first solo-pastorate position. Mrs. Drabble had been at the center of that little maelstrom, too.

Alicia Drabble stared over his shoulder, a faint pink tinting her cheeks. China-blue eyes that rarely met his, golden ringlet curls, porcelain skin, and an air of fragility — nothing at all like her mama, whose physique tended more to the cider barrel shape.

He shook Alicia's limp hand and turned back to her mother. "I do thank you, but I'm afraid I will have to decline once more. I've already accepted an invitation to lunch at the Mackenzie home." And grateful he was, too.

The Drabble matron's face hardened, and the creases at the corners of her lips deepened. "I see." She tugged at the hem of her bodice and shifted her Bible to her other arm. "You do realize your first annual review as our pastor is coming up soon. The district supervisor is a very good friend of mine, and it would pain me to have to tell him you were playing favorites amongst your congregation."

The barb in her voice nicked his conscience, and he did a quick gallop around his social calendar to see if she might be correct. Had he been showing favoritism to some over others? The last thing he wanted or needed was a bad report sent to the home office, and until recently, he'd not feared one. But the drawn-out discussions that bordered on arguments over something as simple as new windows for the church had set up a distant warning gong in the back of his mind. In the front of his mind was the knowledge that his father, as the home office director, would be sure to read any report and know his son wasn't living up to his exceedingly high expectations.

Matilda Mackenzie appeared at his elbow as if she had somehow sensed he could use rescuing. "Silas, we're looking forward to your visit today. David and Karen want to show off the little one and talk about a dedication service here in a few weeks."

Mrs. Drabble's severe expression melted into a smile, and she held wide her arms. "Matilda, so lovely to see you." Embracing the smaller woman, she kissed the air beside Matilda's cheek. "Congratulations on that little granddaughter. I hear she's quite a beauty. I can't wait to see her."

Matilda extricated herself. "Thank you, Beatrice. Karen felt it would be best not to bring the baby out in public for a few weeks. It's been such a cold spring. We'll serve dinner at one, if that suits you, Silas." She patted Silas on the arm and strolled toward the door without waiting for an answer.

Beatrice's lips twitched. "I can never get over parishioners calling a pastor by his first name. I guess it was the way I was brought up, proper and all, but using a pastor's first name . . ." She gave an I-don't-know-what-this-world-is-coming-to shrug.

Silas held in a sigh and vowed to be polite,

long-suffering, patient, enduring all things. . . . "Mrs. Drabble, I did give the adult congregants leave to use my first name if they wanted to."

"And you'll remember I told you I thought it improper. As the spiritual leader of this flock, you can't maintain your dignity and position if you allow people to call you by your given name. If you ask me, even the term pastor is rather . . . common. Reverend" — she traced an arc as if the word could be read across his chest — "is much more ministerial and fitting for the office."

Two young men edged around them, heading for the door. Silas nodded to Kenneth Hayes and his friend. The young man had installed the new windows, and a fine job he'd done, too. Silas didn't miss the black look Beatrice shot Kenneth or the way his shoulders ducked and hunched. Poor Kenneth. She'd criticized and hounded him during the entire construction.

Kenneth's friend elbowed him in the ribs. "You going to the grand opening, or you going to wait?"

He shrugged. "I'll wait a couple weeks till the crowds thin some. Can't say I'm all that interested in the play they're putting on, but I wouldn't mind a gander at the inside of the new theater." Kenneth lifted his chin in greeting to Silas, edging past Alicia who stiffened and lowered her lashes when their arms brushed.

The friend's face split in a grin. "I want to get a gander at that actress. My cousin saw her in Denver this winter. If she's as pretty as he claims, it won't matter what play they're putting on. He said she looked better than a summer sky, and her eyes could make a man feel like he'd been gut-punched."

Silas smiled. All winter the town had buzzed about the new Martin City Theater set to open next week. In a race to keep up with Denver, Leadville, and other Colorado boomtowns, several affluent miners and businessmen had partnered to erect an edifice they felt would elevate Martin City to the status of cultural center. He looked forward to enjoying some of the entertainments himself. It had been a long time since he'd seen a play or listened to an orchestra.

Mrs. Drabble tapped Silas's arm, dragging him back to her. "Don't you agree?"

Uh-oh. He had no idea what she'd even asked him.

Someone whacked Silas on the shoulder. "Great sermon today, Silas. You hit hard and fair."

Silas grinned and shook Jesse Mackenzie's

hand, trying not to wince as his palm compressed in a bear-trap grip. "I just open the Word. I let the Spirit do the teaching and convicting."

"It beats all how you can take a familiar passage like the command for husbands to love their wives like Christ loves the Church and bring out something new I hadn't thought of before."

Mrs. Drabble sniffed. "I would think it would help your ministry immensely, help you preach those types of passages better, if you were married yourself, Reverend Hamilton."

Silas didn't miss her treading heavily on the word *reverend.*

She glared in Jesse's direction. "I believe I mentioned as much to the search committee when Reverend Hamilton was presented to the church as a candidate. We've never had an unmarried minister before, especially not one so young."

Jesse laughed. "Time will cure the young part, and I imagine if we give Silas here a little time, he'll work out the married part, too."

"Not in time for his performance review, I imagine."

"Say" — Jesse checked his pocket watch — "we'd best be moving along. We want to

13

have lunch over by the time the baby wakes from her nap."

Silas didn't miss Mrs. Drabble's parting shot. "It's high time he was married and setting up his own nursery. He owes it to his congregation."

Willow Starr followed her sister Francine up the center aisle of the Martin City Theater. Weariness pulled at her limbs and tightened the band around her forehead, though it felt good to stretch her legs after sitting on the train all afternoon. If only she could escape to the little creek she'd glimpsed from the train window. From long experience, she knew only solitude would allow her to return to the theater refreshed and ready to work.

"At least it's a decent size, though I never would've chosen navy blue for the chairs and drapes. It makes it much too dark in here." Francine poked one of the new, velvet chairs with her folded fan. "Positively saps the light. We'll have to adjust the footlights and our makeup or we'll all look positively ghastly."

Philip shoved his hands into the pockets of his narrow, striped trousers and rocked on his heels. "Hello! 'Alas, poor Yorick!' " His voice filled the empty theater. "Wonderful acoustics."

Francine's mouth pinched. "You're no Edwin Booth. Now *there* is an actor. My mother played opposite him, you know. The greatest production of *Hamlet* ever seen outside the Globe Theater."

Willow smothered a smile as the three stagehands behind Francine pantomimed this well-worn phrase. Her sister brought up her acting pedigree at every opportunity, as if being the daughter of the woman who played Ophelia to Edwin Booth's Hamlet made her a great actress, too.

Francine continued up the aisle, the skirts of her ornate traveling gown falling behind her to a train that brushed the carpeted floor with a whisper of satin on wool. "I see they have ample balcony boxes. After that shack we were booked in at the last town, it's nice to see a place with some class."

Willow separated herself from the gawking actors and wandered over to one of the pillars supporting the balconies above. She leaned against the solid post and closed her eyes, wishing away her headache and anticipating getting settled into her room at the hotel and having some peace and quiet. Finding time to be alone had been particularly difficult lately, and she felt like a rag doll with the sawdust drained out.

"Willow, you're going to ruin your posture slouching like that." Francine sounded so much like their late mother, Willow snapped to attention before she realized what she was doing. "We need to inspect the dressing rooms and see that our costumes have arrived."

Philip Moncrieff made his way through the actors and offered his arm to Willow as she approached. "Allow me." His mouth twisted into an oily sneer under the pencil-thin moustache. With his back to everyone, he didn't bother to hide his bold leer.

Her throat tightened, and she stepped back. Though she'd suspected from the first time she'd seen him that Philip might be trouble, she hadn't anticipated how much. Nearly old enough to be her father, he had made a game of pursuing her this past winter, always covertly, laughing at her blushes and evasions and getting closer and closer to outright insulting behavior.

"Philip?" Francine cut through the chatter. "Let's go see what the dressing rooms look like."

He rolled his eyes, pulled his lips into a pleasant smile, and turned on his heel, but not before winking at Willow and whispering, "Perhaps later, my dear."

She swallowed the distaste on her tongue.

Walking to the stage, she didn't miss the whispers from the rest of the troupe. Her sister's possessive attitude toward Philip was common knowledge. Willow, having no designs on the lecher herself, was grateful. If Francine kept him dancing attendance on her, he wouldn't be free to make things difficult for anyone else.

Willow followed, pausing to caress the velvet curtains. Even in low light the narrow boards of the maple stage gleamed with wax and elbow grease. Her shoes echoed as she crossed in front of the footlight reflectors.

A familiar form slipped into the theater in the back, and she smiled. Clement Nielson, director and friend, and the only person in the troupe with the clout to override her sister's demands. He waved and cupped his ear.

Her shoulders straightened, and she tightened her abdomen. " 'Life appears to me too short to be spent in nursing animosity or registering wrongs.' " The line from their upcoming play, *Jane Eyre,* flowed out to the corners of the auditorium. Though Willow was aware of Francine's snort of disapproval coming from the wings, she didn't acknowledge it.

Clement nodded and made a damping motion.

Willow dropped her voice to a whisper. " 'I am no bird; and no net ensnares me; I am a free human being with an independent will.' "

"Bravo, child." He strode up to the stage, planted his hands on his lean waist, shoving back his jacket, and looked up at her. "I knew this part would be perfect for you."

Francine glided over, a ship in full sail. "Clement, I hope you're not making a dreadful mistake. It isn't too late, you know."

Willow's fingers tightened in the folds of her skirt, waiting for a repetition of the histrionics Francine had gone into when Clement first announced the cast for the upcoming production of *Jane Eyre.* The thrill of being awarded her first starring role had been snuffed under an avalanche of protests, tantrums, and petulant criticism, to the point that Willow had been ready to beg Clement to let her sister take the part.

Especially since creepy Philip would be playing Mr. Rochester. The hours she would spend in his company pretending to be in love with him would surely tax her acting ability to the limit.

"The cast is set, Francine. Willow is more than ready. She'll be a sensation. You've read the reviews from this past winter. Even in her supporting roles she's garnering attention." Clement bounded up the stairs, energetic as always, and touched Willow's chin, lifting it slightly. "I've never seen a more perfect ingenue. With that face, form, and ability, they'll be clamoring for her in New York, San Francisco, Paris, London, Berlin. . . ." He smiled, white teeth flashing, and feathered his fingers through his thin, pale-yellow hair. "I've only held back until now, waiting for a bit of wisdom and serenity to appear in those marvelous gray eyes. She only lacked a bit of maturity to her carriage and voice." He clucked his tongue. "It was that tip-tilted nose. Gamine, pixie-ish, and alluring, but without a bit of maturity to counter it, she appeared too young. Until now."

Willow kept her gaze steady on the director, well used to being discussed as a commodity, an object with pros and cons. With Clement it wasn't personal. He spent a great deal of energy and time cataloging his cast and using everything at his disposal — costumes, lighting, makeup, positioning, props, sets, the lot — to bring out the best performance possible. He knew his actors inside out.

Or so he thought. Clement knew the public her, the actress who could pretend to enjoy the crowds, the demands, all the people pushing and prodding her to do what they wanted. But there was another Willow, intensely private, needing solitude, longing for stability in a life that had them moving every few weeks, longing to put down roots, fall in love, marry, and raise a family.

Only once had she dared to let that part of herself show, had she dared to give voice to her own desires and dreams of love and marriage, and Francine had squashed her dream flatter than dropping a sandbag on an éclair. "Ridiculous. Mother raised us both better than that. The daughters of Isabelle Starr deserve better than to be shackled to a cookstove, caring for the squalling brats of a dirt-poor farmer or miner. She'd turn over in her grave."

Clement clapped his hands, drawing Willow back to the present. "For now, I say we start making ourselves at home. We'll be here for the next two months, so feel free to unpack over at the hotel. Dressing rooms are over there." He waved to the wings. "Name cards are already affixed, and no sniveling as to the assignments." His brown eyes panned the cluster of actors. "Costume trunks should've arrived from the depot by now." He indicated the woman in charge of costuming. "Make sure everything got here in one piece. I'll get together with you and the prop master tomorrow for any last minute issues." He raised his voice. "We'll do a read-through rehearsal tonight at six, so don't be late."

Francine's brilliant green eyes glittered, and her jawline tightened, but she didn't challenge Clement's casting decision further.

Willow followed her off the stage, around the ropes and rigging for the curtains and backdrops, and down a narrow hall to the dressing rooms. She winced at the white card tacked to the center of the first door. WILLOW AND FRANCINE STARR.

Not that she wasn't used to sharing a dressing room with her sister, but to Francine Starr, billing was *everything.* To be listed, even here in this dim hallway, second to her younger sibling . . .

Bracelets clanked but didn't drown out the snort as Francine snatched the card, crumpling it and tossing it to the floor. "Now that we know which room is ours, we don't need the card." She twisted the knob and shoved the door open.

Willow set her features into a pleasant expression and stepped into the dressing room. Clement needn't worry about her acting abilities on stage. Anyone who could pretend to be at peace in the company of Francine Starr in a temper was a fine actress indeed.

TWO

"She's a beauty, just like her mother." Silas cradled Miss Dawn Matilda Mackenzie, gazing down into her tiny face. "You're a blessed man, David." He only hoped he didn't drop her or break her.

David eased himself into a chair in the drawing room, his wide smile creating deep creases in his cheeks. "I try to remember that when she wakes the entire household squawking in the middle of the night." Though blind, he wore a cloak of serenity and satisfaction Silas admired.

David's wife, Karen, slipped out of her shoes and tucked her feet up under the hem of her dress on the settee, glancing ruefully at Silas. "You don't mind if I get comfortable? We've been friends long enough for a little informality." She smiled when he shook his head — faint dark smudges hovered under her eyes. Her hand came up to cover a delicate yawn. "It's been two months since the baby arrived, and I haven't managed a decent night's sleep yet."

Celeste Mackenzie, David and Karen's adopted daughter, sat primly on a footstool beside David. The child wore a spotless pinafore and shiny boots as black as her hair. Her sky-blue eyes, thick lashed and striking, never left the baby's face. Most beautiful of all was her smile.

Only a few weeks ago, Celeste's upper lip had been a ravaged snarl due to a birth defect. Now, after surgery, a thin pink scar showed where repairs had been made. The surgeon had assured her parents the scar should fade in time.

"Are you a big help to your mother?" Silas knew the answer, but he loved to hear Celeste's voice. For so long she'd hidden her mouth behind a scarf and kept her voice to a whisper, speaking only when she had to in a lisp so mangled only those who knew her well could decipher it.

"I try to help her all I can. And Buckford does, too. If I didn't have to go to school, I could help more."

David smiled. "I tried that very argument on mother when Sam was a baby. It didn't work then either. You're going to school, young lady. You're all healed up from surgery, and you start tomorrow."

24

"I heard you were going to finish out the spring term here in Martin City." Silas gingerly shifted the baby so he could pat Celeste on the shoulder. "You don't need to worry. The teacher is very nice, and you'll have Phin and Tick there to introduce you around. Your cousins like the school well enough. You'll soon find yourself with lots of new friends."

The infant squirmed, squeaked, and shoved her fist into her mouth. Smelling faintly of milk and that special brandnewness that only very young babies have, she snuggled into Silas's arms. An empty place in the corner of his heart swelled a notch. What would it be like to hold his own child?

Jesse strode into the room, his presence filling every corner. "How're my best girls?"

Celeste shot off the footstool and ran to him, hugging his waist hard. Jesse put his arm around her shoulders, grinning.

Silas smothered a smile at how Jesse strangled his normally booming voice into a hoarse whisper so as not to scare his granddaughters. "You'd best be careful Matilda doesn't find out you've demoted her in favor of Celeste and the baby."

Matilda entered the room ahead of the butler with a tray of tea. "It wouldn't be news. He's been besotted since the moment grandchildren came into the family. If he isn't fishing with the boys or teaching them to ride, he's having a tea party with Celeste." Warmth shone from her eyes. Though married for thirty years, the Mackenzies displayed a love and affection that didn't seem to have faded or gone stale.

David rubbed his jaw. "Tell me about it. If he buys one more toy, we won't be able to get into the nursery. I can't tell you the number of times I've gone to get the baby from her nap to find Father there ahead of me cooing and babbling and fussing. I had no idea what a mush lived inside the man."

Jesse grinned, unrepentant.

Matilda poured the tea, placing Silas's cup at his elbow. She poured a splash of tea into Celeste's cup and smothered it with a healthy dose of milk, smiling as she gave it to the little girl.

Silas decided to let the tea sit rather than risk trying to drink while holding the baby. "Thank you for inviting me today. Sharing a fine meal with friends would be enough of an inducement, but couple that with a chance to see this new little sweetheart" — Silas bent his head — "and I was all too eager to accept."

"Mrs. Drabble wasn't pleased you'd escaped her hospitality again." Matilda sipped her tea.

Silas sighed and squelched the first thought that leaped to his tongue, since while truthful, it wasn't edifying in the least. "I'll call on her sometime this week to make amends. I've had conflicts of schedule every time she's extended an invitation lately."

"Lots going on in town this spring. Yesterday I noticed they were putting up some posters in front of the new theater." Karen leaned back into the sofa and closed her eyes. "David, don't forget about the tickets."

"I haven't forgotten." David patted her leg. "Silas, I've acquired a box at the theater for the Friday after next. Not for opening night, I'm afraid, since I have to head to Denver and won't be back in time. Mother and Father and Sam and Ellie will be joining Karen and me, and we hoped you'd be able to come, too."

"I'd like that very much." Pleasure warmed him at being included. Though sometimes he kicked against the demands of his job encroaching on his personal time, he had to admit evenings at home with only the cat to talk to weren't all that stimulating. A chance to spend an evening in good company watching an excellent play . . . something to anticipate.

"Good." David yawned, apologized, and yawned again.

Dawn squirmed and snuffled, and Jesse leaped out of his chair. "I'll take her upstairs to the nursery. C'mon, Celeste, you can help me." He scooped the baby up and strode toward the staircase, Celeste trotting at his side.

Matilda shook her head. "He's just looking for an excuse to rock her and spoil her some more. I'm going to have a hard time keeping him from invading Denver every week or so to check on her when you go home this summer."

Silas chuckled. Sipping his tea, he glanced at David and Karen on the settee, both with eyes closed. "I think we've lost them to sleep. I'd best be taking my leave, Matilda. Thank you for an excellent meal, and I look forward to the play."

She took his cup and stood. "Do you want me to send around for the carriage to take you home?"

"No, I think I'll walk. Some fresh air and exercise are just what I need."

Striding along the road a short time later, he tried to thrust aside the feelings of discontent and longing nibbling at his heart. Over the past several months, he'd been aware of a growing sense of something missing from his life, of a void wanting to be filled. Being with the Mackenzies both alleviated and accentuated the sensation. It was impossible to be lonely while in their company, and yet the closeness shared by Jesse and Matilda, David and Karen, especially with the addition of that new baby, made him aware of his solitary existence in a new way.

Stripping off his tie, he thrust it into his pocket and shrugged out of his suit coat. Still feeling confined, he unbuttoned his vest and left it open and loosened the top couple of buttons at his collar. When he got home, he'd get out of this starched shirt and into his favorite plaid flannel, a relic from his seminary days when he'd worked on the docks in Upper Sandusky to put himself through school.

An unseasonably warm breeze scudded along the road, kicking up puffs of dust, and to his left, Martin Creek burbled and chuckled, throwing back sparkles and reflections that illuminated the undersides of the trees hanging over the water. The beauty of God's creation moved him to a prayer he often uttered.

Lord, thank You for the people of my flock. Please help me to lead them to know You better and to seek Your will. Give me wisdom to minister to them and to be a good pastor.

Would he be a better pastor if he were married? Did he owe it to his congregation to find himself a wife and start a family? Would it matter to his performance review? The denomination preferred married ministers, but they didn't require it.

He shrugged and shifted his jacket to his other arm. There were several nice young ladies in his congregation who had let him know, through means subtle and overt, they wouldn't be averse to his calling upon them as a suitor, and yet not a one of them evoked a response in him beyond that of their pastor.

He'd always believed he'd know the minute he spotted her — the woman who would make his life complete, the woman who would balance out his shortcomings, bolster his strengths, complement him in every way. There would be a connection between them that neither could deny, a sense of rightness, of inevitability. Was he being stubborn and fanciful waiting for an ideal that wouldn't materialize, or was he right in not settling for something less?

The idea of sharing the intimacies of marriage — not just the physical intimacies, but the spiritual, emotional, mental intimacies — with someone without feeling that spark of attraction and exhilaration was unthinkable.

Renewed resolve to wait — not to be pushed into marriage by Mrs. Drabble, or the denomination, or even his own loneliness and disquiet — flowed through him. He wouldn't settle for second best. He would wait until God brought the right girl into his life.

With his mind at peace, he turned off the road and wended his way toward the creek bed. The sun still had some distance to travel before the mountains to the west obscured it and cast long dusky shadows. Time for a little rock hunting.

Reaching the water, he kept his eyes on the stones under the purling eddies. When an interesting color or shape caught his eye, he plunged his hand into the icy water to retrieve it. The best went into his handkerchief; the rest went back into the stream. He'd almost reached the outskirts of Martin City when movement upstream drew his attention.

A young woman sat on a flat rock at the edge of the stream, her knees tucked up and her head tipped back to soak in the sunshine. She spread her arms in a graceful arc, lifting her hands overhead. Her loose sleeves fell away to her elbows, revealing slender white arms. In a lithe movement, she rose and balanced on the rock, executing a pirouette, a musical laugh flowing out over the sound of the water. Her light skirts belled with her circling, and her hair, her beautiful hair, fell in glossy brown ripples around her shoulders.

Silas stilled, captivated. Such freedom and abandon, such joy in her surroundings — he instinctively smiled. When had he last met someone so carefree?

She began to sing — light, gentle, and dreamy — her voice a perfect match to her fluid movements.

"It was many and many a year ago,
In a kingdom by the sea,
That a maiden there lived whom you may
    know
By the name of Annabel Lee;
And this maiden she lived with no other
    thought
Than to love and be loved by me."

As if he had no control over his tongue, his voice rose and blended with hers on the lines of the popular poem-turned-song.

She dropped her arms and stopped mid-pirouette, and his gaze collided with the most incredible pair of gray eyes he'd ever seen.

The shock of finding she wasn't alone nearly propelled Willow off the rock and into the water. She stumbled, caught herself for a moment, and overbalanced again. A small shriek shot from her lips as she pinwheeled her arms, flailing the air to keep her footing.

Just when she knew she was headed into the icy creek, iron bands closed around her waist and hauled her landward. In a flurry of arms and legs, she and her rescuer tumbled to the grassy verge and landed with a thud. The stranger broke her fall, and the air whooshed out of his lungs.

She lay for a moment imprisoned in his arms, panting and stunned at this turn of events. Her cheek rested against his chest, and the solid thrum of his heartbeats reassured her that she hadn't killed him. Realization flooded her. She was lying in the arms of a strange man!

Scrambling up and away, she managed to elbow him in the stomach and squash his arm before righting herself. "I'm so sorry." A hank of hair slid over her forehead and obscured him from view. She scooped it aside, bunched her curls at the base of her neck, and tugged it all to lie in an untidy pile on her shoulder. "Are you hurt?"

The man propped himself on his elbows and grinned. The most perfect, symmetrical smile with white, even teeth. Warmth flooded his brown eyes, and his rumpled hair fell onto his forehead. She couldn't stop staring at so much handsomeness.

"I think I'll survive. I'm sorry I startled you. Good thing we found a soft place to land. Another yard to the right or left and we'd have landed on boulders." His deep, mellow voice rolled over her like the warmth from a stove on a cold day. He sat up and brushed at the dirt and twigs clinging to his shoulders and sleeves. A healthy grass stain decorated one of his cuffs. "Hmm, Estelle isn't going to like that."

His mutter jarred her. Estelle? Willow edged backward. She shouldn't be noticing how handsome he was, or how strong, or how gallant his rescue of her was when he was a married man. The heat that had rushed into her cheeks when she first realized she wasn't alone intensified until she thought she might burst into flames.

"I'm so sorry. Will your wife be angry?" Her lips felt stiff and uncooperative, and she grasped for her professional demeanor. The cloak of protection that usually came

to her aid in tense situations proved uncooperative as well.

His eyebrows arched. "My wife?"

"Estelle? Who won't like that you've
stained your clothes?"

He laughed, and her heart tripped at the
deep rumbly velvety sound. "Estelle isn't
my wife. She's my housekeeper, and she is
always after me to keep my Sunday shirts
clean."

Relief all out of proportion made Willow
weak, and she joined in his laughter. "You
really *are* in trouble then. I am sorry."

"No worry, and anyway, I should be
apologizing to you. I'm the one who scared
you, belting out those lyrics like that." He
cast about him as if looking for something.
"Be right back."

With a fluid twist he leaped to his feet and
jogged downstream.

How had he managed to cover so much
ground to rescue her in time?

She took stock of her appearance. A dead
leaf curled into her hair, and she'd ripped
the lace edging on one of her sleeves. Lovely.

Francine would have a conniption if she
heard about this. Imagine one of Isabelle
Starr's daughters caught so disheveled in
public. *Your image, my dear. It's all an
actress has.*

35

Her rescuer returned with a suit jacket over his shoulder. The white edges of a handkerchief poked from his other hand. "I was sure I'd lost these when I dropped everything. It all happened so quickly. I thought you were going to get an icy bath for sure. This water comes down from up there." He pointed with his thumb up to the peaks to the north where each rugged edifice bore a shawl of snow. "This creek never gets what you could call warm, but right now, it's dangerously frigid."

She shivered, grateful not to have had a dunking. "I shouldn't have been acting so silly, twirling out there on that rock. I might've gone in with or without being startled."

Opening his handkerchief for a moment, she caught a peek at a handful of rocks before he shoved everything into his pants pocket. *Rocks?*

"Actually, it was refreshing to see someone so carefree. Quite the most charming thing I've encountered since coming to Colorado." His smile and the light in his brown eyes set off a fluttering under her ribs. "I'm only sorry I butted in and scared you."

She wasn't. She'd be quite content to be affected like this every day of her life. When she realized she was staring again, she let her lashes fall. He must think her a simple-minded idiot. And he wouldn't be far wrong, considering how he'd come across her.

"As much as I have enjoyed meeting you" — he glanced at the sky and grimaced — "time's marching on, and I have an appointment soon I can't break. I'd be happy to walk you home on my way."

Willow stiffened and sucked in a gasp. How had it gotten so late? Francine would have plenty to say if she was late for the read-through; and if she showed up in her current disordered state, she'd never hear the end of it. "I'm sorry, I have to go as well. Thank you for rescuing me."

She lifted her hem and scrambled up the bank toward the road, realizing as she fled that she hadn't asked his name.

THREE

"What's the matter with you, Willow? Get your head out of the clouds." Francine snapped shut her powder compact and set it down with some force on the dressing table. "You might be enamored of being the star of this play, but let me tell you, you're not ready, and I doubt you ever will be. *I* should be playing Jane." Picking up her hairbrush, she primped the heavy auburn ringlets lying on her shoulder. "If Clement had an ounce of directorial sense left in his head, he would see you haven't developed enough as an actress to give a convincing performance."

Willow stifled a sigh and went back to studying her script. Her sister had a tendency to get stuck on a conversational waterwheel, turning and turning and pouring out the same cold, damp accusations. Protesting wouldn't stop the flow.

"You're not listening to me." The brush

collided with the tabletop, and Francine's imperious eyes met hers in the three mirror panes — each from a slightly different angle and each pair of black-lashed daggers summing Willow up and finding her wanting.

"I'm trying to learn these lines so I'll be ready for rehearsal." She checked the enamel clock on the shelf. "It's almost time."

"See, this is exactly what I'm talking about. An actress" — Francine drew in a deep breath and spread one arm wide, jangling the bracelets on her wrist — "doesn't 'learn lines.' She *becomes* the character."

How many times had their mother said the same thing?

Francine rouged her lips. "You haven't the faintest clue how to play Jane Eyre. Mother saw to it we had the best acting classes, diction and singing lessons; and anyone with an ounce of sense knows that I'm the better actress. Clement is just being difficult, giving you the lead."

Willow held her tongue.

A knock interrupted the tirade. "Rehearsal."

Willow thankfully closed the notebook containing her script and rose, letting her heavy silk skirt settle around her and making sure her posture couldn't be caviled at. "Are you ready?"

"Of course." Francine stood, checked her appearance once more, and swept out ahead of Willow.

Scooping up Francine's notebook, Willow propped it on her hip with her own and headed to the stage. All the warning signs of a major storm were brewing, and she didn't look forward to a rehearsal with Francine in this mood.

Though she was only a few moments behind everyone else in arriving, she could still feel the half-triumphant, half-accusatory glare Francine shot her way. Clement stood at his lectern marking up his script while several actors waited. Francine swept across the stage and seated herself in the most comfortable chair.

Philip Moncrieff sidled up to Willow. "You look lovely, my dear." His oleaginous voice slid over her. "Clement seems to be of the opinion you and I need some more rehearsing in order to be fully prepared for opening night." Turning his back to the director, he rubbed his hand down Willow's arm. "I'd be happy to rehearse with you whenever you'd like. Especially our more tender scenes."

Willow snatched her arm from his grasp

and edged around him.

Clement tapped his pencil to get everyone's attention. "I want to work first on act 2, scene 3. Philip, if you could watch your pacing here. You're rushing a bit, and Francine, though you have a major part in this scene, it won't do for you to obscure the leads. I need you to stay near the settee. You're such a commanding presence and so lovely, you'll draw too much attention away from Willow and Philip if you walk clear across the stage."

Willow had to admire how Clement handled her sister. Through flattery and cajoling, he got her to do his bidding while making her think it was her idea the whole time.

The next three hours taxed Willow's patience to the limit. Nothing she did satisfied Francine, though Clement encouraged her efforts and interpretation and praised her at every turn.

True to form, Francine hadn't bothered to work on her lines much yet, relying heavily on the poor young girl who had the woeful job of being "on-book" for rehearsals, shouting out "Line!" at frequent intervals, and snapping her fingers until the girl supplied the next line.

Oddly enough, on the two occasions when

41

Willow stumbled over a line, Francine supplied it perfectly without waiting for the prompt from the wings.

Still, things were coming together, and Francine Starr was too proud to go onstage for a performance without knowing her own part well. There would be crazed cramming, bouts of tears, and histrionics in the run-up to opening night, but she would appear serene and in command once the footlights were lit.

Clement finally called an end to rehearsal, and Willow sagged into a chair. Acting left her exhilarated and exhausted, a confusing combination that required solitude to sort out. While the rest of the cast and crew filed out of the auditorium, Willow let the ensuing quiet bathe her soul.

Her mind drifted to the place it wanted to be, back beside the stream talking to the extraordinary man who was never far from her thoughts these days. Though she'd returned to the creek twice in the last week, she hadn't caught sight of him. Every time she walked through the hotel lobby or down the main street of Martin City, she searched for his face, but so far they'd not crossed paths again. She couldn't get him out of her head, and the more she remembered his face, his voice, his laugh, and the way it had felt to be held in his arms, the more she longed to see him again, if only to confirm he was as truly wonderful as she'd made him out to be.

Footsteps sounded behind her, and before she could turn, a hand came down on her shoulder, clamping and kneading the base of her neck. "I thought I'd find you here. You're tense. Let me help you."

She shot out of her chair like she'd been snake bit, her script crashing to the floorboards and pages fanning and flapping. "Don't, Philip. I don't like you touching me."

He laughed, and the predatory look on his face was such a contrast to the image she had in her mind of her gallant rescuer of a few days ago, she flinched.

"That's because you're such an innocent. Don't you know that touch-me-not air you wear drives all men mad? It begs a real man to break down those icy walls and touch the fire he knows burns there."

Ignoring his customary flair for the dramatic, she sought to cut him down once and for all. "You wouldn't know a real man if he walked up and shook your hand. If you don't leave me alone, I'm going to complain to Clement." This direst of threats didn't even make him pause.

"If you do, he'll assume we won't be able to carry off our parts on stage as passionate and star-crossed lovers. He's likely to bounce you right out of your role and put Francine in your place." He spoke with such assurance, Willow wondered if he'd already broached the subject with the director. "I've worked with Clement a long time. He won't remove me as Mr. Rochester, because" — Philip held up one finger — "I'm perfect for the role, and there isn't anyone else in the troupe who can play the role, especially not three days from opening night. You, on the other hand, could be ousted like that." He snapped is fingers. "Francine has your lines down perfectly. She's practically salivating."

Frustrated with the undercurrents, the petty squabbles and jealousy, and Philip's slimy manipulation, Willow stooped and gathered her papers. "If you don't leave me alone, she'll get her wish. I'll walk out of this production so fast your head will spin. And then where will you be? What do you think the critics will say, and the public?"

He flinched. The posters around town promised Willow as Jane Eyre, and there were two Denver critics already in town awaiting Friday night. A change in the lead role at this late date would spell disaster, and he had to know it.

Without a word, he turned on his heel and stalked away, leaving Willow alone in the vast auditorium. As she tidied her papers and studied the chandeliers, the rows of seats, and the ornate balcony boxes, she realized she could walk away from all of this without a backward glance. If only she had some place to go.

Silas pinched the bridge of his nose and tried once more to get the meeting back on track. Committees were one of the most difficult parts of his job. While he knew the need for counsel and getting people involved in the decision making and running of the church, committees leeched time and energy, often created rifts where none would've existed, and taxed his patience.

His board of elders — both of them — and the deacons and deaconesses sat in the front two rows of pews, while he sat in a straight-backed chair before them. His Bible and the meeting itinerary lay on a small writing table at his elbow, and his watch lay open beside them, the hands creeping toward the top of the hour.

"Jesse, could you give us the financial report?" Money and the church. The combination made his stomach tighten. No wonder Jesus addressed money so often in His parables and teaching. No subject got believers worked up quite as quickly as cash . . . unless it was the lack of it.

Jesse Mackenzie shuffled a few pieces of paper and cleared his throat before launching into a detailing of expenses set against the tithes and offerings that had come in the last month. Silas fought to keep his mind on business as various ideas were put forth regarding acquiring an organ and whether to increase the giving to the China Inland Mission.

Inevitably, they reached the line item MARTIN CITY ORPHANAGE. Dissention abounded on this issue, and as he had feared, the center aisle divided the yeas from the nays.

"We're not debating whether or not to help the new orphanage, but rather in what capacity. Mr. Mackenzie has the floor right now. There will be opportunity for discussion as soon as he presents his findings." He gave this gentle reminder when Larry Horton and Beatrice Drabble scowled, and Beatrice looked set to start another diatribe on the orphanage. She set her mouth, reminding Silas of a mule his father had once owned, and crossed her arms, waiting her turn.

The discussion continued, and Silas listened with only half an ear. The rest of his attention drifted to the one thing he couldn't seem to get his mind off of.

The girl.

Once more he gave himself a mental kick for not at least getting her name. His search for her had proven fruitless over the past week. Not that he'd had a lot of time to devote to looking. Church business, sermon preparation, teaching his midweek boys' class, visitation, an unexpected trip to a neighboring town — his duties filled his time, and until now he'd embraced them with eagerness.

But that was before he'd rescued an adorable sprite with lively gray eyes and a nose that tilted up at the tip just enough to save her from other-worldly perfection. Her grace and clear soprano voice, her laughter and the delightful way the color rose in her cheeks — he remembered every second of their encounter.

Not to mention the feel of her in his arms, and how his heart had raced with her head pillowed against his chest.

He dragged his mind away. A man had no right to let his thoughts dwell on a woman that way when they weren't even courting.

Courting. He swallowed, and the hunger

to know more about her, to find out if she was even free to be courted, tugged at him.

"I don't see why you're all so eager for one ministry to drain the resources of the church in this manner." Mrs. Drabble's voice cut across his thoughts and brought him back to the meeting at hand.

Jesse Mackenzie leaned forward and planted his elbow on the pew ahead of him, resting his cheek on his fist. "Mrs. Drabble, the board of elders brought this motion before the congregation months ago. You voted for it yourself. It's our obligation as Christians to take care of widows and orphans."

"I agree, but I voted yes assuming our contribution would be merely financial. Adding the orphanage to our missions giving is one thing. Expecting me to oversee volunteers, fund-raisers, and I don't know what else . . ." She dabbed her neck with her lacy handkerchief. "It's the windows all over again. People rush to say they want something done, and the work of bringing it about falls upon my shoulders."

Mr. Meeker, who served alongside Jesse as a church elder, cleared his throat and offered as meekly as his name implied, "Mrs. Drabble, if I remember correctly, you declared if the church was going to be headstrong and insist upon having stained glass windows, you were the only one of the congregation qualified to see the task done. You took over the entire project. We wanted to help you, but you said you didn't need help."

Her lips puckered, and her nostrils flared. "I was the only one who had experience with ordering materials from abroad. Of course I saw it as my duty to shoulder the burden once the board had rushed into the decision."

Silas rapped the tabletop lightly. "Everyone, please, can we stay on the topic at hand? Mrs. Drabble, the windows are beautiful. You chose well, and we all rested more easily knowing the project was in your capable hands." He shot Jesse a warning glance. Mrs. Drabble might be at times a chore, but she was one of the most capable and organized women he'd ever met. When she took on a task, it got done, and heaven help anyone who stood in her way. "That's why we feel you are just the person to be in charge of the orphanage outreach. No one here could see to the needs of these poor unfortunates as well as you."

A flush came to her cheeks. The wrinkles beside her eyes deepened, and she dabbed at her neck once again.

Her husband, a languid, quiet man, nodded and patted her hand. The Drabbles owned the largest mercantile in Martin City, supplying everything from canned goods to chandeliers.

"Beatrice." Heads turned to Matilda Mackenzie, seated beside her husband. "If it will be of help to you, I'd be happy to assist. I'm in rather a unique position as both a board member of the orphanage and a deaconess of this church. Together I'm sure we can find a balance that benefits the orphanage and doesn't tax the church's resources, financial or physical, too much."

Silas called down mental blessings on Matilda for being willing to serve with Beatrice. Then he noticed the tightness around Matilda's mouth. She would bear with Beatrice if it meant bettering the lot of the orphans who had just taken up residence in the new Martin City Children's Home, but she was well aware it would be an uphill battle.

"There is one last thing on the agenda." Silas tapped together a folder of papers. "These questionnaires arrived from the home office this week. Each of the elders and deacons — not the deaconesses, I'm afraid — are asked to fill them out, seal them in the envelopes provided, and drop them in the mail by the end of the month. This is the first step in my performance review."

He handed the folder over the railing to Jesse, who took a set of clipped pages and passed the folder back. "I won't ever see these questionnaires, so you can feel free to be honest. In about six weeks, the district supervisor will arrive to interview the board and me and to sit in on at least one church service." Silas's heart beat faster. "I would appreciate your prayers for myself and for each other in this matter."

The meeting finally adjourned, and he motioned for the Mackenzies to stay behind for a moment so he could thank them privately. But before he could, there was the Drabble gauntlet to run.

She pressed her fingers into his palm. "I'll make sure Walter gets that paperwork filled out and sent in promptly. He has a tendency to let things like that wait until the last minute if I don't prod him along. I have to say, you're looking much too thin these days, Reverend Hamilton. You're not ill, are you? You're working too hard and not getting enough home cooking. I insist you share our evening meal tomorrow night. It won't do for our pastor to be looking gaunt

51

and overtired when the district supervisor visits."

"I'd be delighted, Mrs. Drabble." He accepted, glad for her sake his schedule was open. "Nothing is better than an excellent meal in congenial company. It's nice of you to be concerned about my health."

She beamed. "Actually, it was Alicia who brought it up. She's so caring that way, always looking out for everyone else. Such a giving, compassionate girl. She'll make a man a wonderful helpmeet, don't you think?"

Pitfalls yawned everywhere around this woman. "A daughter to be proud of."

More beaming, and a proprietary gleam in her eye that made his throat go dry. "Tomorrow at six. Don't be late now."

Jesse waited until she was out of earshot then chuckled. "You better be careful, or you'll wake up one day and find you've Beatrice Drabble for a mother-in-law."

Silas gave a shaky grin. "Perish the thought." He held out his hand to Matilda. "Thank you for jumping in when you did. You'll be rewarded in heaven."

Jesse's laugh boomed out. "It will have to be in heaven, because I doubt working with Beatrice here on earth will be rewarding."

Though he echoed Jesse's sentiment, his

conscience knocked on his heart. "When I'm tempted to complain about awkward parishioners, God always reminds me He loves them as much as He loves me, and I have more than a few shortcomings of my own that need attention."

"You're right." Jesse gave him a sheepish smile. "We've all got our faults. Although as far as Beatrice is concerned, though you might have some minor issues that need your attention, so far you've only one major flaw."

"Being single?" He rubbed his palm on the back of his neck.

"There's a quick way to fix the situation. If you get married, she won't have anything to complain about."

"Jesse" — Matilda tugged on his arm — "Silas shouldn't get married just to stifle critics. When he meets the right girl, I'm sure he'll be only too eager to wed. Until then, it's his business. Sometimes you barge in where angels wouldn't tiptoe." An indulgent smile took the sting out of her chiding.

"Maybe, but the truth remains. If he wants to get Beatrice off his back, all he's got to do is get married."

FOUR

By the third curtain call, with the audience appearing to have lost little steam, Willow knew they had a hit on their hands. The entire cast bowed again to uproarious applause, and though Francine would probably later remark on the behavior as vulgar, the men filling the cheaper seats stomped and whistled.

Philip gripped her hand so tightly her fingers tingled. She had to give him credit. He played his role as the masterful, brooding, mercurial Mr. Rochester with skill and flair. The consummate professional on stage. Too bad that professionalism disintegrated the moment he stepped into the wings.

The house lights brightened, bringing the audience into view for the first time. Though she had told herself not to be silly, she couldn't help searching the sea of gas-lit faces for the one that had occupied her thoughts and even her dreams this week. Curtsying, waving, acknowledging their appreciation over and over, she looked for him. Her chest squeezed when she didn't find him.

Stop it, Willow. Be patient. There's such a crush in here, you probably couldn't find your own sister in the crowd.

This thought did make her smile, since Francine considered it her duty to make sure *everyone* saw her.

Clement leaped onto the stage carrying an armful of red roses. She kept her smile in place, familiar with this opening night ritual, but he didn't stop in front of Francine, as was his custom. This time he breezed past and stopped before her. When he laid the flowers in her arms, the audience erupted again. "Congratulations, my dear. You are a sensation."

Pleased, bemused, and surprised, she cradled the fragrant blossoms. She hoped her makeup hid the blush she knew colored her cheeks. "Thank you, Clement."

He placed his hands on her shoulders and kissed her brow to more raucous applause. "You deserve every rose, every laud, every praise. I have never seen a more gifted performance." He patted her hand. "Now, go get out of your costume and into a party dress. The reception will begin as soon as you arrive."

The opening night gala. A ballroom festooned with streamers and hothouse flowers, a laden buffet table, and hundreds of guests. As she threaded her way back to the dressing room, weariness seeped through her and a faint pounding began behind her eyes. If tonight's party followed the familiar pattern, it would be approaching dawn before she could be alone and sift through all the thoughts tumbling in her head.

"Help me with my dress." Francine, always the last to leave the stage, marched into the dressing room. "Hurry up. We're expected."

Foolish of her to hope for some small word of praise or approbation for a good performance, and yet, the armor she'd grown around her heart where her sister was concerned proved to have a few vulnerable spots still. Francine had taken up where their mother had left off, and Willow saw no end to the criticisms and petty jealousies in sight.

"I must say, I enjoyed my role as Mrs. Fairfax more than I thought I would." Francine dampened a cloth and removed the stage makeup from her face in wide swipes.

Willow said nothing. She unhooked the

back of Francine's costume and stepped away to see to changing her own clothes.

"Of course Clement had to present you with the flowers. He had no choice, since you were billed as the lead, but really, you're going to have to work on your role. Wooden doesn't begin to describe you. You could've been reading a menu rather than responding to the love of your life. Philip positively carried you through the proposal scene."

Francine continued her sideways picking all through redressing her hair and reapplying her makeup. Willow could find it in her to pity her sister, so concerned with the outside shell and, nearing thirty, forever in pitched battle against her archenemy, time.

"Hurry up. We don't want to keep people waiting. Help me with my gown." Francine held her arms up so Willow could slip the silvery silk and lace evening gown over her head. The gaslight winked on the crystals sewn into the bodice.

"You look beautiful." Willow straightened a few stray wisps of hair. "Are you going to wear the diamonds?"

"Of course." Francine checked her reflection. "I wouldn't be caught dead on opening night without my jewelry." She opened her case and withdrew the necklace their mother had bequeathed to her. Securing it behind her neck, she dipped in again for several rings, bracelets, and a pair of teardrop earrings that caught the light.

Willow fastened her sister's gown up the back and turned so Francine could help her with the removal of her own costume. Stepping into a white evening gown of chiffon over satin, she held her breath while Francine jerked at the buttons.

Please don't tear the fabric.

She finished, and Willow pulled the pins from her hair, letting the brown mass tumble out of the severe style necessary for her role as Jane. Brushing so quickly her hair crackled, she then pinned it up loosely on her head, encouraging a few ringlets to fall over one shoulder and pinning an ostrich feather and crystal clip to the back of her head. She lifted her single strand of pearls, also a bequest from her mother, and clasped them about her throat.

"You aren't even done with your makeup." Francine dabbed on perfume and checked her reflection once again.

"It won't take me long. You could go ahead."

A snort. "You'd like that, wouldn't you? Arriving all alone and stealing the limelight?"

"I only didn't want to hold you up." She

wiped off the makeup she'd worn on stage. Though it looked ghastly in the candlelight of the dressing room, the heavy paint was necessary in the lighting of the theater to make her look natural. Without the eye-rouge, base, and powder, she would appear so pale and undefined as to be almost face-less.

But a ballroom full of theater guests was a different audience, and she could dispense with the heavy makeup. She took only a moment to powder her face and smooth her eyebrows before taking up her beaded evening purse and cloak, squaring her shoulders to brave the crowd. She swirled the black velvet cloak over her shoulders and tied the strings at her throat.

Her heart thumped against her ribs as she followed Francine from the theater to the hotel next door and into the ballroom reserved for the party. Perhaps *he* would be there, and she would have a name to match the handsome face.

Music and light poured from the ball-room, and people laughed and talked, help-ing themselves to the buffet and reliving the performance.

Clement met them at the door. "My dears, your public awaits. I've already spoken to several critics, and they're all in raptures." His hands never stopped moving, fluttering over his hair, tugging at his tie, ducking into his pockets, only to be withdrawn immediately. "Let me take you in."

Francine took his arm. "Philip will bring Willow." She raised her chin and flicked a glance at Philip over Clement's shoulder.

Willow hid her grimace and stood back from the doorway to allow Francine to enter alone. A smattering of applause filled the air.

"She's choked with envy." Philip tugged on his white gloves. "And no small wonder. You did play your part beautifully." He offered his elbow. "Come, my darling Jane Eyre. As your beloved Rochester, I shall see you into the party."

She rebelled inwardly at being called *his* anything but untied the strings on her cloak and let it fall from her shoulders.

A hotel servant took the garment, and Philip let out a low whistle. "I say, that dress is striking. You'll upstage every woman in the room." Again he held out his arm.

Laying her fingertips lightly on his sleeve, she put on a calm, pleasant expression and prepared to act the part of the ingenue Clement wanted her to be.

The moment she stepped over the threshold, the room erupted into applause. Bodies pressed close, shaking her hand, showering her with compliments, and each encounter sapped a little more of her energy. Philip and Francine imprisoned her between them.

Several people called her Jane, a testament to her acting skill that they actually thought of her in terms of the character, but it left her hollow — as if she weren't a real person, as if they didn't see the real her.

Francine accepted every plaudit as if it belonged to her, and Willow was more than happy to let her have the attention. When she could finally escape the reception line, she found a quiet corner to sip a cup of punch in and study the crowd.

He wasn't here. She really shouldn't have expected him, and yet though her mind told her heart over and over he shouldn't be this special to her — not after one chance encounter — her heart refused to be sensible.

"My dear, that dress becomes you delightfully," Clement said as he approached.

"Thank you. It's one Francine ordered, but when it came, she thought it made her look pale."

"Well, on you it is enchanting. You look like an angel." His knowing, pale eyes roved her face. "I'm not blind, Willow, nor is the rest of the cast and crew. They see how

Francine treats you."

She swallowed, touched by his concern. "It isn't that bad. She just cares so much. Being the center of attention means everything to her. It's all she has, all she knows."

"The theater is all any of us knows. None of us could walk away unscathed."

His words struck her. Was the theater all she had? Could she walk away unscathed?

Silas rested his fishing pole on his shoulder and dangled his tackle box from his fingertips. Shutting the door on the parsonage and his sermon notes for next Sunday, he couldn't help the tickle of anticipation at playing the truant for an afternoon by the creek.

A warm spring breeze, so welcome after the bitter winter just past, brushed across his face. He breathed deeply, hitched the strap on the bag holding his lunch higher onto his shoulder, and set out for Martin Creek.

With each step, he shed the responsibilities and cares of his flock and allowed himself to relax and embrace the beautiful day. Following the burbling stream, he descended the hillside toward the rock-strewn oxbow where rainbow trout darted in the crystal water.

Would she be there?

He chided himself for allowing his thoughts to return once more to the young woman. His attempts at concentration since meeting her had been paltry at best. The fact that he'd been unable to locate her since then had driven him to distraction. If he could only see her once more, convince himself his memory had played him false, that she wasn't as perfectly beautiful as he remembered, then perhaps he could get her out of his mind and focus on his job as a pastor.

And that was the only reason his steps quickened as he reached the place where he'd last seen her.

She was there.

He had to blink to make sure his mind wasn't tricking him.

She sat on the flat rock, her arms wrapped around her up-drawn knees. A wide-brimmed hat shaded her face, and she had her brown hair tucked up, revealing her slender neck and the delicate line of her jaw.

His foot loosened a pebble that skipped and bounced down to the water, and the sound caused her to turn toward him. Even from a dozen paces her gray eyes sucked his breath away.

His memory hadn't played him false.

"Good after—" His voice rumbled in his chest, sounding rusty and hoarse. Silas cleared his throat and tried again. "Good afternoon."

Her welcoming smile made his chest feel like the sun had risen just under his heart. Satisfaction, as if he'd finally found something he'd been looking for all his life, washed over him.

"Good afternoon. I see you came prepared to fish me out if I fell in today." She pointed to his gear.

Laughing all out of proportion to her small joke, he approached her and set his equipment on the bank. "I'm playing the truant from work this afternoon. It's much too nice to stay inside."

"I agree. I escaped for a while myself. Sometimes I just need to get away from everyone."

"Am I intruding? I'll go if you like." *Please say no. Please ask me to stay.* The plea rose up so strongly he almost voiced the words aloud.

"I'd be glad of your company." A blush pinked her cheeks, and her lashes fell. "I'm sorry I had to rush away before. I was late, and my . . . employers won't tolerate lateness."

She lifted a pine branch from the rock

64

beside her and trailed it in the water. Resin from the broken tip created a rainbow pattern on top of the water, and sunshine threw brilliant reflections up under her hat brim and lighted her face with ever-changing dapples.

The burning desire to know everything about this woman surged through him, but he sensed her reserve and cautioned himself to go slowly. "I wasn't offended. Your devotion to your employers is admirable." Seating himself a respectable distance away on another sun-warmed rock, he studied her profile. "It's nice we're both able to take an afternoon off every once in a while. I know I was getting weary battling the books. The boys I was preparing a lesson for would much rather be out climbing trees and playing ducks and drakes."

"Ducks and drakes?" Her tip-tilted nose wrinkled. "I've not heard of that."

"It's another name for skipping stones." He cast about his feet and located a flat stone the size of a silver dollar. He brushed it off and tossed it in his palm, testing the weight. "This is a perfect skipping stone. Watch." Silas stood and hurled the stone, watching in satisfaction when it bounced across the water half a dozen times before disappearing beneath the surface.

Her delighted laughter rippled through him.

She tossed her stick into the stream, rose, and dusted her hands. "I've never skipped a stone in my life. Show me again."

He found another rock, flicked it at the stream, and winced when it ricocheted off a boulder with a *clack*. "Hmm, not so good." He grimaced. "You try it. Find a good flat rock. Those work the best."

She found a stone and tossed it into the stream. *Plop.* "Well, that was unspectacular. What did I do wrong?" A tiny crease appeared above the bridge of her nose.

He found another flat stone. This time his toss netted him eight skips.

She tried twice more with poor results, and each time the concentration on her face deepened and her determination to master the skill became more pronounced.

"You need to throw more from the side. Make the rock fly parallel to the water for as long as possible." He flipped a stone across the surface of the creek. "And don't forget, I've had a lot of practice at this."

Another of her attempts ended in failure and a splash that wet the hem of her dress. "I'm never going to get this." She blew out a breath and went to searching for another stone.

"Here, let me help you." Silas stepped up onto the rock beside her and reached behind her to take her right hand in his. This close to her, he couldn't help but notice the porcelain quality of her skin and the bird-delicate bones of her hands and wrists. Giving her plenty of time to stop him, he eased his left hand around her waist to steady her. "Draw the stone back like this" — he suited action to words — "and throw it like this." He pantomimed, slowly propelling her hand forward on a flat plane. "One, two, three." On three, the stone sailed through the air, skimmed the water, flipped, skipped, bounced, and after a half-dozen hops, plopped into the water.

"We did it!" She turned in his arms, gave a little hop, and hugged him, the light of triumph gleaming in her eyes.

He returned her exuberant embrace, thrilling at the feel of her in his arms.

"Thank you." She leaned back and seemed to realize what she'd done. She let her hands drop from his shoulders and stepped back. Pink surged into her cheeks to replace the glow of accomplishment.

"Careful." He kept hold of her elbows, lest she tumble into the stream in her haste to put some distance between them.

"I'm sorry. I overstepped." She gripped

her fingers together at her waist and gave him a good view of the top of her hat.

Reluctantly, he let go of her. "You did nothing of the sort." He put his finger under her chin and raised her face until she had to look at him.

Confusion clouded those gray depths, and an awareness — the same awareness he'd felt from the moment he'd first seen her — that he was a man, she was a woman, and something strong drew them to one another.

He smiled, trying to coax a response from her. "I'm hungry. Will you share my lunch with me?"

She grasped at this as if he'd thrown her a lifeline in the midst of her storm of uncertainty. "I'd be happy to."

He took her hand to help her to the bank but let it go right away. He didn't want to scare her, and the power of his feelings, so fresh and new, surprised him. "I have sandwiches and apples." Digging in his rucksack, he produced the napkin-wrapped bundles. He shrugged out of his coat and spread it on a patch of grass for her. "There. Don't want your dress to get muddy."

"I suppose I should've had a care for that before I sat out there on that rock, but the water seemed to be calling to me, and I just had to get closer to those ripples."

Silas handed her a sandwich. "I'll say grace."

She stilled for a moment and nodded, bowing her head.

"Lord, thank You for Your beautiful creation, for sending spring after winter to remind us of how You are faithful to keep Your promises. Bless this food to our nourishment. Amen."

"Amen," she whispered.

He bit into the thick bread and sliced ham. Bless Estelle for baking a ham for him this week. He swallowed carefully. "I had hoped to see you in church this past Sunday. Martin City only has one house of worship, so I was sure you'd be there." He winced, hoping his eagerness didn't come across as an accusation. For all he knew, she'd been indisposed, or her employer had required her presence on Sunday morning.

She shrugged. "Oh, I almost never go to church."

Cold shock poured over him so he had to check to make sure he hadn't slipped into the water, and he realized how far along the path of his future his thoughts had already raced. The *one* command God required of His children when it came to choosing people to commit to for life, the *only* requirement He stipulated was they be not unequally yoked, believer to unbeliever. It had never entered his mind that this beautiful girl who had stolen his imagination and was on the verge of stealing his heart wouldn't know Jesus as her Savior. His potential bride had suddenly become his mission field.

She appeared unaware of the blow she'd dealt him, taking a delicate bite of her apple and dabbing at her lips with the corner of her napkin. The similarity between the temptation of Eve and his own temptation now yawning before him didn't pass him by without notice.

"Of course, that doesn't mean I'm a total heathen." She scanned the aspens on the far bank. "My father was a man of deep faith, and he passed that on to me. Why, if it wasn't for my faith in God's saving grace, I think I would lose all hope in this life and certainly my hope for the next."

The muscles in his stomach loosened a fraction. "So you know Jesus as your Savior, but you don't go to church?"

"Oh, I'd like to, but my schedule rarely allows it." She tucked her bottom lip behind her teeth, and her eyes clouded. He sensed her backing away from his questions. Glancing at the sky, she wrapped her half-eaten lunch back into the napkin. "I'm sorry, but

I have to go."

"Wait." He shot to his feet, tumbling his sandwich to the ground. His apple bounced right into the stream and bobbed away. Before she could escape, he grabbed her wrist. "Please, there's one more thing I have to know about you."

"I really do need to be getting along before I'm missed."

"I can't possibly let you go without telling you my name and asking for yours. My name is Silas Hamilton." He let go of her wrist and held out his hand, praying she would take it.

She hesitated and shook her head as if to chase away a thought. Slipping her fingers into his palm, she clasped his hand and solemnly studied his face. "My name is Willow. Willow Starr." Without another word, she took her leave, slipping through the white aspen trunks and disappearing over the brow of the hill.

He stood on the bank staring after her. Willow Starr. Where had he heard that name before?

FIVE

Silas, his hair still damp from his hasty bath, walked along Center Street toward the brightly lit theater, but his mind was still on his encounter with Willow Starr at the stream that afternoon. Her name was perfect, unique, descriptive, fitting. Anticipation lengthened his stride. An evening in the company of the Mackenzies never failed to stimulate and cheer him, and there was always the faint chance he might run into Miss Starr tonight. Martin City had precious few entertainments suitable for a young lady, so it was highly likely she would attend the performance at least once.

There was an idea. He grinned. The next time he saw Miss Starr he would invite her to the theater. First he needed to find the Mackenzies.

Quite a crowd gathered around the doors to the theater, and more people descended from carriages, wagons, and buggies. Being tall, Silas had an advantage, and soon he spotted Jesse Mackenzie's thick head of white hair.

"Glad you found us. Quite a crush." Jesse shook Silas's hand. "If David hadn't reserved a box for us a couple weeks ago, I doubt we'd have gotten tickets for tonight."

David smiled and shrugged. Karen tucked her hand into his elbow and sighed.

"Aren't you looking forward to this evening?" Silas studied her.

Before she could answer, David laughed and patted her hand. "She's just worried about the baby. First evening out since Dawn was born." He slipped his arm around her waist. "Now Karen, you promised you would try to have a good time. You know Buckford's more than capable of tending her. He practically pushed us out the front door; he was so anxious to get to rock her all he wanted without you fretting that she would be spoiled. Celeste will help with the baby's bath, and everything will be just fine."

Karen blushed but fought back. "And who was it who went upstairs to check on the girls three times before we left? *And* made sure everyone would know where we would be? *And* made sure someone would be on hand to run for the doctor and the theater if anyone so much as sneezed?"

"All right, all right." David hugged her close to his side. "We're both anxious parents, but we're going to try to have a pleasant time this evening and not talk about the kids the entire night. Although Mother and Dad might not mind, we don't want to bore Silas."

A fist pummeled Silas's shoulder, and he turned to see Sam and Ellie Mackenzie. David's younger brother grinned. "Hey, there, padre. Glad you could come tonight."

Silas shook Sam's hand and then Ellie's. He'd been pleased to officiate at their wedding this past Christmas, and if anything, they appeared to be even more in love than they were just a few months ago. "Are Phin and Tick all set for Sunday afternoon?"

Ellie nodded. "They've spoken of little else since they got your invitation. You'll have your hands full taking all the church boys on a picnic. Are you sure you don't want some of us to come along and help corral them? I know from experience how exhausting they can be."

The doors opened, and people began entering the theater. Jesse handed over the tickets and ushered everyone to the reserved box.

Silas barely had time to assure Ellie he

could handle things before he was directed to a chair. "They've done this place up properly." He took in the chandeliers, the velvet draperies, and the gilded woodwork.

A small orchestra played from the pit in front of the stage, and a swarm of conversation buzzed as people found their seats.

Jesse took the chair next to Silas. "I'm glad you could come tonight. I worry about you."

Silas started and drew his attention away from the decor. "Me? Whatever for?"

Jesse's bushy white eyebrows lowered. "I think you're working too hard. You already pile a lot of the load on yourself, and on top of that, we've got this visit from the district office coming up."

The coils that wrapped around his windpipe every time he thought about the performance review tightened, and Silas had to force himself to relax. "I'm the pastor. That goes along with the job. If I don't do it, nobody else will."

"You see, that's where you're wrong." Jesse leaned to the side as Matilda, on the other side of him, shifted in her chair to speak to Sam and Ellie behind her. "You've got to delegate more. You're preaching, teaching Sunday school, not to mention taking the church boys on outings, doing repairs around the church, and last week, didn't I catch you with a mop and a bucket sluicing down the front steps?"

"Well yes, but —"

"No buts. Add that to your visitation, leading the singing, directing board meetings, and lending a hand wherever you see a fellow in need, and you're doing too much. You'll get stretched so thin you'll wear through." Solicitude laced his words and colored his eyes.

"Jesse, I do appreciate the concern, but all those things need doing. I can't just tell the sick folks I won't come see them, and I can't expect anyone else to stand up in the pulpit for me." He spread his hands.

Jesse grunted and crossed his arms. "Maybe not, but there are a lot of things you do that someone else could do for you. You have elders and deacons. You need to delegate."

"I do. Bernice and Matilda are overseeing the orphanage project."

"And how much oversight will you have? You'll be following up after them to make sure things are going smoothly and getting done, which is just as much work as doing it yourself. It's time you let go and let others have the joy of serving. You delegate, but then you wind up spending as much time or energy — or even more — on checking up after folks than if you'd done the task yourself."

Matilda leaned forward. "Jesse, is this really the time to chastise Silas? I thought we invited him out to get him away from work."

Sheepishly Jesse patted her hand. "Of course, dear. Silas, she's right. We brought you here so you could relax, and what do I do but bend your ear with shoptalk?"

Karen tapped Silas on the shoulder and handed him a playbill. "*Jane Eyre* is one of my favorite novels. I'm so glad we get to see a performance, though I can't imagine how they can fit it all in. The book is so big it would make a great doorstop. I hear the actress playing Jane is fabulous."

Silas took the playbill, but his thoughts tumbled over what Jesse had said. Was he failing to delegate? Did his elders think he didn't trust them to do their jobs? As always, his analytical mind picked up advice or criticism and turned it over and over, studying, weighing, evaluating. Would any of these things surface in the reports to the home office?

Flipping the program face up, his heart somersaulted. Willow's beautiful gray eyes looked at him, and her name blazed an inch-high just under the name of the play.

Willow Starr as Jane Eyre. Of course! That's where he'd heard of her.

He read every word of the playbill, even the advertisements, then carefully folded the program so her picture wouldn't be creased and tucked the pages into his suit coat just over his heart. He tried to remind himself he was a grown man and should have better control of his faculties, but his pulse leaped and his mind raced at the thought of seeing her on the stage tonight. All thoughts of church and responsibilities and delegating fled.

Thankfully the Mackenzies weren't given to chatting during the play, because Silas wouldn't have been able to concentrate on anything they were saying. From the moment Willow stepped into the glow from the footlights, he was completely captivated. She was nothing short of magnificent. Graceful, appealing, gentle, and yet powerful; she mesmerized him.

Only one thing jarred him throughout the performance, and heat swirled through his ears, and his chest got prickly tight when he realized it. Jane Eyre was in love with Edward Rochester. And Willow played the part perfectly. When the actor portraying Rochester took Willow into his arms, it was all Silas could do not to leap over the balcony onto the stage and rip the man's hands away. He shifted in his seat, tried to relax the grip he had on his knees, and told himself he was being foolish in the extreme.

When the curtain came down on the last act, Silas found himself standing, clapping until his hands stung. The house lights went up as the actors came onto the stage to receive their applause from an appreciative audience. Men in the cheaper seats whistled and stomped. Some threw their hats into the air.

Silas had eyes only for Willow. The footlights picked out the pretty flush on her cheeks and shone in her eyes. He braced his thighs on the half wall in front of him and clapped and clapped.

She looked up, went still, and put out her hand to shade herself from the bright footlights. Her eyes met his and locked. One of the lines from the play came back to him, about an invisible cord strung between two hearts. A week ago he would've scoffed at such an idea. Too fanciful for a grown man. And yet it was as if a warm, golden, vibrating strand connected them. Everything around him disappeared, and there was only Willow. She seemed to feel it, too, for she stood perfectly still, staring up at him.

Jesse clapped him on the shoulder, breaking the spell. "That was something. And there's more. We've been invited to meet the cast at a little reception at the hotel next door."

Silas couldn't stop grinning. And he couldn't wait to tell Willow how amazing he thought she was.

"You were rather uninspiring tonight." Francine Starr wiped the heavy color from her lips. "I can't think what got into you. Clement must be out of his mind to keep you in the lead role. I'm only glad Mother isn't here to see what's become of all those acting lessons she paid for." She sighed and dipped her fingers into a rouge pot.

Willow, pinning up her heavy brown hair, met Francine's eyes in her mirror and gave in to the rebellion flickering in her middle. "You should never be glad Mother isn't here. Anyway, the audience seemed to like my performance well enough." One in particular. Just the memory of the pleasure and pride on Silas's face was enough to make her breath hitch and cause her to feel reckless. Though she was glad she hadn't known he was in the audience during the play or it might've made her too nervous to remember her lines.

"This ignorant audience doesn't know sic

'em from come 'ere about acting. They'd applaud if you walked on stage and recited the state capitals." Yanking on her gloves and shoving her rings onto her fingers, Francine glared. "What else can you expect from a backwater place like Martin City? Unschooled laborers and artistic cretins. I should be in New York or San Francisco, not stuck here playing bit parts in a nowhere town."

The spark of rebellion against her sister's tirades fanned into a candle flame. "Have you spoken to Clement about this? Perhaps he'd let you out of your contract."

"You'd like that, wouldn't you? Me clearing out and leaving the way open for you to take all the starring roles?" Francine pushed herself up from the dressing table and loomed over Willow. "I intend to regain my leading lady status, and I'll do it with *this* company. Clement Neilson will see reason, or he might find himself without a job. He has risen to his current position on the Starr family's shoulders. First Mother, then me. Without that cache, he wouldn't be able to get a directing job in a two-bit minstrel show. Everyone in this cast knows I should be playing the lead, and if I so much as snap my fingers, there will be a revolt." Her eyes bored into Willow. "I could shut down this show in a trice."

What she said was true. Most of the performers knew Francine's good side was the safest place to be, and she'd been the leading female since Mother died so suddenly almost five years ago. If Francine wanted to make things difficult, she could, and most of the cast would side with her out of a sense of self-preservation.

And if Francine sailed into the party in her current temper, more heads would roll than during the French Revolution, but before Willow could pour some oil on the water of her sister's wrath, Francine swept out of the room, slamming the door in her wake. "Don't be late!" This parting shot came through the flimsy door, followed by the angry tapping of footsteps heading down the hall.

Willow checked her appearance one last time, twisting the curl lying on her shoulder and straightening her necklace. Guilt rose up and snarled with the feeling that she was trapped in a situation she could never change. Francine would *never* change.

Lord, forgive me for baiting her. Please help me to be patient, not to return her sharp words. And Lord, I'd really love it if he was at the reception tonight.

Was it wrong to pray that Silas would

come to the reception? She didn't know but hoped God didn't think so.

Silas had been in the best box in the house, so he must have some money or influence in this town. Surely he'd been invited to tonight's reception.

A light rap sounded on the door. "Willow, are you ready?" Clement.

She opened the door and smiled. "All set. Is there going to be a big crowd tonight?"

"Not too big. Nothing like it was opening night." He tucked her hand into his arm. "Before we go in, I've gathered the cast together for a special announcement." Leading her toward the stage, his eyes picked up the light from the wall lamps and magnified it. His step was jaunty, and a smile played under his precise moustache. They reached the stage where the actors and actresses clustered.

"Really, Clement." Francine's voice pierced the conversations around her and brought them to a halt. "Is now the best time for this? We've got people waiting at the hotel."

"I won't take long, and I think you'll all want to hear this." He removed Willow's hand from his elbow but kept hold of her fingers. "I've received word of a wonderful opportunity. A tremendous offer has been made to this troupe to appear at the Union Station Theater in New York City for the summer production of *Romeo and Juliet*." He swung Willow's hand and rocked onto the balls of his feet, beaming. "A twelve-week run in New York City."

A jolt went through the crowd, and eyes lit up. Smiles abounded, and everyone spoke at once. Francine stood front and center, biting her bottom lip, her eyes sparkling more than the diamonds at her throat. "*Romeo and Juliet?* New York City. Oh Clement, that's wonderful. I can't wait. I wish we were already finished here so we could leave right now." She spread her arms wide and twirled in a circle. "And at the Union Station Theater."

It was moments like these Willow treasured, when Francine forgot to be haughty or petty and let her natural love of life burst through. Her large blue eyes shone, and her porcelain skin glowed with life and excitement. This was the sister Willow remembered best from her childhood, before Mother died, before Francine became consumed with taking her place in the acting troupe. Before the ten-year age gap between them began to dwindle in significance.

"I'm going to be a wonderful Juliet." Francine clasped her hands under her chin and fluttered her lashes. " 'O Romeo, Romeo, wherefore art thou, Romeo?' "

Clement cleared his throat. "Actually, Francine, the offer stipulates that Willow be cast as Juliet. They've read the early reviews, and one of the theater representatives was in Denver last month to see the final performance we had there. They were very taken with Willow and want her in New York as soon as possible."

A fountain of warm pleasure bubbled up in Willow's chest. "Really?" Her mind whirled with the possibilities. To play Juliet in New York City. It didn't get any better than that for an actress.

"What?" Francine's incredulous voice silenced conversation and sucked the warmth out of Willow. "You're jesting, aren't you?"

"I'm not." Clement's voice held a bit of steel. "The offer is very specific. They want Willow in the lead role. Without her consent, the offer is void. Everything hinges on her."

Willow blinked. "They want me? For Juliet?"

A calculating expression flitted across Francine's face before she assumed a smile. "Willow, what an honor. I'm so happy for you." She came forward, gripped Willow's upper arms, and kissed the air beside her cheek. Willow held in a wince at the fierceness of Francine's hold and tried not to shiver at the brittleness in her eyes. They would talk about this later for sure.

Clement continued. "Let's get over to the reception before our guests wonder what's become of us. And for the moment, I would suggest we keep all this under wraps until the contracts are signed." He motioned toward the front doors but held Willow back when she lifted her hem to go. Francine threw a look back over her shoulder, but Clement waved her on. When they were alone, he rubbed his chin. "You need to consider getting an agent or manager to see to your career."

"Francine manages my career."

"That's been fine up until now, but you're destined for bigger things than Francine can deal with. You have no idea your own potential, Willow. Francine will never let your light shine brighter than her own, and hers is waning with each new season. You're on the cusp of an amazing career, bigger than hers, bigger than anything you ever imagined. You'll be famous, and your name will be on everyone's lips. You'll have more money and prestige than you can imagine.

It's all there waiting for you. And you'll need someone to guide you, someone to manage things, especially the money you'll be earning. And if you will consider it, I'd like to present my services. I know this business, and I would have your best interests at heart. Would you consider it, making me your manager?"

The life he described — the fame, the fortune — while exciting, didn't seem real, as if he were speaking of another person. While she was flattered and pleased at the offer, her heart didn't skip the way she thought it should. Any rational mind would leap at this chance, right?

He laughed. "I can see I've taken your breath away. But Willow, your mother was a good friend to me, and she asked me to look after you girls."

"This has been a surprise." Her cautious nature exerted itself. "Do they need an answer right away? I'd like a little time to think about it, to sit down with you and go over some of the details, perhaps read the contract myself before I make up my mind."

Tucking her hand into his elbow, he led her into the hotel. "We have some time. A few weeks even, but I'm sure you'll find everything straightforward. You think about it. It's all there waiting for you, and I'll help you any way I can."

Moments later, stepping into the reception room, Willow searched for Silas. She finally found him beyond the punch table.

And he wasn't alone. Her spine stiffened. Half a dozen young women surrounded him, eyelashes flicking faster than their painted fans. His white smile flashed as he bent his head to hear what one of them had to say.

Before she was ready, his glance met hers across the room. The same swooping, tingling feeling that had assaulted her when she first saw him in the balcony swept over her again obliterating Clement's news and the possibilities it offered. She took several breaths, but each seemed to clog in her throat. Someone at her side spoke to her, but she heard nothing but the beating of her heart.

Silas excused himself and threaded his way through the crowd until he stood before her. "I had no idea you were an actress. You were exquisite. Really amazing." His rich, velvety voice flowed over her.

A warm glow at his praise fizzed up and filled her cheeks. "Thank you. You really liked it?"

As if it were the most natural thing in the world, he took her hand, threading his fingers through hers and squeezing. "I was enthralled from the first scene."

Francine appeared at Willow's shoulder, her brow as serene as it had been stormy before. "Willow, darling, you made it at last." She appeared to notice Silas for the first time, and her lashes fluttered while her lips pursed into a small pout. "Hello." She held out her be-ringed hand. "I'm Francine Starr, and you are?"

Disquiet tiptoed up Willow's spine. She'd not told anyone about meeting Silas on the riverbank, not wanting to share for fear of rubbing some of the bloom off.

Francine had a predatory gleam and was putting herself out to be charming. Would Silas, like so many others, be drawn to her great beauty?

Silas bowed and took Francine's offered hand. "Silas Hamilton. A pleasure, Miss Starr. I enjoyed your performance very much this evening."

"My, my, Mr. Hamilton, you have a wonderful voice, so deep and full. Have you ever considered the stage?" Francine kept hold of Silas's hand, and Willow forced herself not to react.

He smiled, and deep creases formed on his cheeks. Not quite dimples, but almost. "I guess you could say I've done my share of public speaking, but I'm no actor. I'll leave that to professionals such as Willow and yourself. Your performances were so compelling, I lost all track of time and place tonight. Of course that happens every time I'm in Willow's company." Though he spoke to Francine, his warm gaze locked with Willow's.

Francine arched one carefully sculpted eyebrow. "That is, of course, the goal of any actress, to captivate her audience to the exclusion of all else." Her glance went from Willow to Silas and back again, and Willow could almost hear the wheels turning.

A large, gray-headed man clapped Silas on the shoulder. "Fine performance tonight."

Silas introduced him as Mr. Mackenzie and went on to make introductions for the rest of his party.

Willow smiled and talked and played her part, but in the back of her mind the uneasiness lingered, fostered by the appraising gleam in her sister's eyes.

Six

The evening after seeing the play, Silas fought to concentrate on his sermon notes. Every time he relaxed for an instant, his mind wandered to Willow. Because he found this a pleasant pursuit, he found his mind relaxing all too frequently.

She was exquisite. Everything about her appealed to him. And to find she was as talented as she was sweet and beautiful . . .

His chest swelled, and his mouth stretched into the ridiculous grin he'd spied on his face every time he looked in the mirror lately. Only the knowledge he had a sermon to prepare for the morning kept him from attending the theater again tonight.

His black-and-white tomcat hopped up onto the desk, crinkling papers and scattering notes. He sniffed the sermon notes and flopped down across Silas's open Bible, yawning and showing a lot of sharp white teeth and pink tongue.

"Come on. The sermon can't be that boring, Sherman." Silas cupped the furry head, smiling at the rumbling purr deep in the cat's chest.

The cat regarded him with green eyes before falling to licking his snowy paws. Silas propped his elbows on the desk and planted his chin on his fists. "I know. I should be working, but it's hard to concentrate."

A knock sounded on the side door. Grateful for the interruption, Silas went to open it.

"Kenneth, hello. What brings you out tonight?"

The young man stood on the stoop, his hat brim crushed in his fists. "Evening, pastor. I saw your light on. Hope you don't mind me dropping in like this." He shifted his weight from foot to foot.

Silas stood back. "Of course not. My door is always open. I'm happy to see you. Though Sherman is a good listener, he isn't much of a conversationalist." He waved to where the cat lolled on the desk. "Come in."

Kenneth Hayes shuffled in, shoulders drooping.

Silas ran through what he knew about the young man and couldn't come up with a ready reason for his distress, but even his short time in the pastorate had taught him to be prepared for anything. What he saw with parishioners wasn't necessarily what he got.

"Have a seat." He directed the young man to the chairs before the cold fireplace. Kenneth was so ill at ease, having Silas sit behind his desk might scare him off altogether. Even now as he lowered himself onto the chair he looked about ready to bolt. "Would you like some coffee? I can brew up a pot in a jiffy."

"No, I'm fine." He tried to smooth out the creases in his hat, then rubbed his palms down his thighs one at a time. He swallowed hard.

Silas sat across from him. Leaning back, he relaxed hoping Kenneth could do the same.

Sherman dropped off the desk and came over to investigate the visitor. When Kenneth leaned down to scratch the cat's ears, Sherman ducked and moved away to sit on the cold hearth. He wrapped his tail around his feet and went still as a statue.

"Don't mind him. He's a bit antisocial. You'd think a cat living in the parsonage would learn some hospitality, but I haven't managed to teach him yet." Silas changed the subject. "I heard you got promoted over at the Mackenzie mine. Congratulations. Shift manager, isn't it?"

"That's right. Pay increase and day shift." Kenneth couldn't seem to find anywhere to look for long, and he avoided Silas's gaze completely.

Silas decided to jump right in. "What's bothering you? You'll probably feel better if you get it off your chest."

The young man's eyes widened, and his look collided with Silas's for an instant before dropping to the floor between his boots. "I guess you could say I have some girl trouble."

Silas nodded. "Girls do have a way of tying a fellow up in knots."

"This girl could give lessons." He fisted his hands and tapped on the arm of the chair. "I've never been so snarled up. She loves me. I know she does."

"And I take it you feel the same?"

Kenneth nodded, his shoulders slumping. "More than I can say. I can't stop thinking about her. I want to spend every minute with her, and I want to tell the world she's mine."

Silas blinked. Kenneth had summed up rather neatly the way Silas was beginning to feel about Willow. "What's holding you back?"

"She is. It's like she's ashamed of me or something. I want to go to her father and ask permission to court her, but she won't let me. Says she knows her folks won't say yes."

"What objection would they have?" Silas frowned. Kenneth was a fine, upstanding young man with good prospects. He had a good job, came to church regularly, and Silas had never heard of him getting into any kind of trouble.

"I'm not good enough, I guess. I thought getting promoted at the mine might change her mind, but she's standing firm." He sighed.

"Maybe I could help persuade her parents if you told me who she was."

Kenneth shook his head. "Naw, there's nothing you can do. She wouldn't like it if she knew I was here talking to you about it, but I'm going crazy. I had to talk to someone."

"If you aren't calling on the girl socially, where do you see her?"

A flush mottled his face, and he cleared his throat.

"I take it you've been together when her parents don't know?" Silas kept his voice as neutral as possible, wanting Kenneth to see the wrong without having to be bashed over the head with it.

"I know. It's gotten to the point where she's lying to get out of the house."

Silas pursed his lips, considering. "I can appreciate how you feel, being in love, wanting to be with someone. But you have to realize that a relationship based on lies and sneaking around is on rocky ground. She's put you in a bad position by not letting you declare your intentions, and you've put her in a bad place by encouraging her to be untruthful."

Kenneth rubbed the back of his neck and nodded. "I know."

"And you know you have one of two choices to make this right?" Silas leaned forward and put his elbows on his thighs, clasping his hands loosely. "You either have to go to her father and declare your intentions, or you have to stop seeing this girl. Nothing good will come from your continuing to meet in secret. You've already compromised this young girl's reputation by seeing her without her parents' permission."

"There's one other choice." Kenneth mumbled the words.

"Oh?"

"We could elope, just run off and get married. Her folks couldn't say no to me if the deal was already done." A defiant light sparked in Kenneth's eyes. His chin came up, and he gripped his knees.

Silas took a moment to marshal his thoughts and select his words. "That's pretty rash. I know you feel desperate right now, but I would caution you to think this through. If this girl still lives at home, then she's under her father's protection. It is her obligation to honor him. You don't even know if your suit would be denied. Before you do something as drastic and permanent as getting married in secret, it would be best if you talked to her father man-to-man. How would you feel if it were your daughter? Would you want her to run off and get married, or would you want to sit down and talk things out?"

The starch drained out of Kenneth, and he sagged into the chair. "You're right. You're not telling me anything I haven't told myself a hundred times. I guess I just needed to hear it from someone else. If someone ran off with my daughter, I'd hunt him down and fill him full of buckshot."

"Maybe you two are worried about nothing. Maybe her folks will like you just fine."

"I think they're aiming higher for their daughter than a simple shift manager."

"Who's to say you'll stop at shift manager? You've got great potential. The Mackenzies already see it, promoting you so quickly. I have a feeling, if you put your mind to it, you could own and operate your own mine before too long. Don't sell yourself short."

Kenneth shrugged and rose. "I've taken up enough of your time. Thanks for listening."

"Before you go, can we pray about this?" Silas invited Kenneth to sit once more. "I think we'll both feel better if we take it to the Lord."

At Kenneth's nod, Silas bowed his head. "Dear Lord, You know what's on Kenneth's heart. You know how much he loves this girl and wants to be with her, but You also know he wants to do what is right, what You want him to do. I pray You would give him courage to talk to this girl's father, and that if it is Your will, her father would consent to Kenneth courting his daughter. In all of this, we want to glorify You, and we ask for wisdom and for Your will to be made plain. Amen."

"Amen."

When Silas closed the door and returned to his sermon notes, he had to move Sherman off his Bible once more. The cat sat on the corner of the desk, staring at him unblinkingly.

Silas picked up his pencil and bent over his papers, but the cat's unnerving stare made the hair on the back of his neck itch. Finally he threw down his writing utensil. "Fine, you don't have to say it. I know."

Sherman gave one, slow blink.

"I know I need to ask permission to court Willow. It's hypocritical to tell Kenneth what he needs to do to make things right when I've been lax myself. I'll tend to it Monday morning."

Willow kept her head lowered, hoping to slip into the church without being recognized. She stifled a yawn, wishing she could've skipped the reception last night. Falling into bed exhausted at three in the morning was no way to prepare for Sunday worship.

Organ music filled the room, and great blocks of colorful light fell across the congregation from the beautiful windows.

Willow found a seat near the back and placed her Bible in her lap. Worshipping with other believers after such a long absence felt like a favorite shawl wrapping around her. *I'm sorry I've neglected coming to church for so long, Lord. Please forgive me.*

She raised her head just a bit and watched her fellow worshippers from under the edge of her swooping hat brim. Silas must be here somewhere. He'd mentioned church on more than one occasion. She studied the backs of the men in front of her and took surreptitious peeks at those on either side. The place was full. Perhaps he was up near the front. She spied the Mackenzie family, Silas's friends who had brought him to the theater. Perhaps he was sitting with them. Craning her neck slightly, she tried to see, but too many people blocked her way. Short of standing up and making a fool of herself, she had little hope of finding him. She'd have to wait for the service to conclude.

Focus on worship. That's why you're here, not to gawk after Silas.

A side door on the platform opened, and a tall man slipped in. Willow's breath caught in her throat. Though he had his back turned to her to shut the door, she knew in an instant it was Silas. He must be a deacon or something. Perhaps he was reading scripture before the pastor took the pulpit. Pleasure that he would be such an active member of the church warmed her insides. No wonder he was curious as to her church background.

"Please rise and open your hymnals to

100

song fifty-four." His deep voice filled the room. He seemed so comfortable up front; he must help out with the services often. She could hardly wait to hear his singing voice, hoping it was as rich and mellow as his speaking voice.

Fabric swished and pages rustled as the congregation found the right song. And when Silas began to sing, Willow wasn't disappointed. His voice reached her over everyone else's, and she wanted to close her eyes and savor the sound. Guilt at her distraction flew in on swift wings, and she found her place in the hymnal.

After the singing Silas invited them to join him in prayer. He spoke from the heart, his words sincere as he asked God's blessing on the congregation and their time of worship and on the reading of God's Word.

"Today, I'd like to begin a series of sermons on living a godly life. I'd like to open the Word with you and see what God has to say about our hearts and how they affect our actions. The text for today comes from Romans, chapter seven."

Realization swept over Willow, bringing numbness. Silas wasn't just helping with the service. He was the preacher. Her mind hop-skipped, trying to sort the ramifications of his occupation. Though she hadn't pegged him as a preacher, it certainly fit with his demeanor, the caring look in his eyes. But did it fit with the thoughts she'd had about him, the stirrings of romantic notions that had colored her world since she first met him?

Onionskin pages whispered, and Silas paused so everyone could find the passage. He read the chapter with conviction and feeling, and Willow's skin tingled. Such authority in his voice, such power.

"Isn't this just like us? Don't we often suffer the same affliction as the apostle Paul?" Silas scanned the crowd. "The good deeds we want to do we don't do, and the bad deeds we don't want to do are exactly what we find ourselves doing."

Drawn in by the power of his sermon, she forgot where she was, focusing on the truths revealed, immersing herself in once again sharing the fellowship of a church. His description of the struggle against sin mesmerized her. She tucked her lower lip in and pondered his words.

"We forget that as believers we are dead to sin, that sin no longer has the power to control us. We don't *have* to sin, even though we often behave as if we do."

The sermon ended all too quickly for Willow. Why hadn't she seen it before? The power and conviction behind Silas's preaching showed he was born to this calling. He couldn't be anything but a preacher. She was so proud of him that she wanted to stand and applaud.

As everyone rose for the closing hymn, his eyes locked with hers. That familiar and yet strange sensation of being deeply connected to one another made her skin tingle. She responded to his broad smile with one of her own, suddenly eager for the service to be over so she could tell him how wonderful his preaching was.

And yet, when the service ended, Willow hung back, trying to remain inconspicuous until the majority of the parishioners had greeted Silas and exited the church. Several people nodded and said hello to her. The Mackenzies greeted her on their way out. Silas glanced at her several times, smiling, asking her with his eyes to wait.

At last the crowd thinned to an expectant group of boys near the door. Silas came toward her, hands outstretched. "You came."

She returned the pressure of his fingers, unable to quell the joy bubbling through her. "It was a wonderful service."

"Are we going to go now?" The plaintive cry came from a small, towheaded boy with rosy cheeks and pale blue eyes. "You said we could go right after church."

"Just a minute, Tick." Silas turned back to Willow.

"You have to go?" She tried to hide her disappointment and feared she failed.

His hands tightened on hers. "The boys and I are having a picnic and doing some fishing this afternoon. It's a reward for all their hard work in Sunday school. Every last one of them has memorized three different Psalms and the Ten Commandments this winter." He didn't sound as enthused as the boys, and she hoped it was because he didn't want to leave her any more than she wanted him to go.

But duty called, and he must answer. She nodded. "Sounds like fun. I hope you all have a good time."

"Say, why don't you come with us? The theater is closed on Sundays, isn't it? You can spend the afternoon with me and the boys and show off your newfound rock-skipping skills."

She glanced at the children. The younger ones didn't seem to mind, but the oldest one — tall, thin, and with a hank of black hair hanging over his forehead — rolled his eyes, shoved his hands in his pockets, and sighed.

"Phin, do you have any objections?" Silas asked the boy.

For a moment he looked as if he wanted to protest, but in the end he shrugged as if he didn't care one way or the other and herded the rest of the boys out the door.

She tucked her hand into Silas's offered arm. "I'd be delighted."

SEVEN

Silas's blood hummed in his veins, and he knew he was wearing that ridiculous grin again, but he couldn't seem to help it and, truth be told, didn't really want to. Sunshine bathed the world in a yellow glow, and at the center of that world was Willow. The speed with which she'd captured his heart still amazed him, and yet it seemed inevitable, too.

The boys scampered ahead, their high voices piping skyward through the trees. Phin carried fishing poles, while Tick carried the bait bucket. The other three boys, the Hebig brothers, tussled, threw sticks and rocks, and chased one another like puppies.

"Estelle packed enough food for an army." Silas lifted the basket he carried in his left hand. Willow held his right arm, and he could feel every one of her fingers through his shirtsleeve, though she touched him lightly.

She clasped the picnic blanket to her middle. "Thank you for inviting me. I've never been on a picnic before."

"Never?"

"No. Theater life means a lot of moving and schedules and performance halls, not sunshine and fresh air and blue skies."

The wistfulness in her voice caught at Silas. "Then I'm glad you get to experience your first picnic with me. I'm an expert."

"Really? How did you become an expert?"

"I grew up in Upper Sandusky, Ohio, on the shores of Lake Erie. My mother loved to go down to the shore and picnic, and we went dozens of times each summer."

She tilted her head as if trying to picture him as a boy, scampering along the shoreline with wind-tousled hair and rolled-up pants.

He could almost smell the lake and hear the scrape and shush of the water as it rolled in and broke on the shore. And he could hear his mother's laughter, which, like the warmer temperatures, always came out in the spring and disappeared in the fall.

"How about here?" Phin popped up at Silas's elbow. "Is this a sunny enough spot?"

"Here is perfect."

The boys fell to work spreading the plaid, wool blanket and opening the hamper. Apples, rolls, fried chicken, cookies. In an incredibly short amount of time, they devoured their share and took off for the stream.

Willow, only halfway through her meal, blinked after their retreating backs. "They'd give a hoard of locusts a run for their money."

"They're boys. You wait. They'll be back before long looking for something to eat."

"They can't possibly. After all that food?"

"It's true. Estelle knows boys." He lifted a towel from the basket and revealed a pan of turnovers. "After they've run around for a while, climbed a few trees, and fought a few imaginary battles, they'll be back and ravenous."

"They seem like nice boys. I have to admit, I can't find any resemblance between Phin and Tick. Where did he get such an unusual name, anyway?"

Silas smiled. "You won't find a resemblance because Phin and Tick are adopted. Tick got his nickname because he always sticks so close to Phin. Though now that he's got a stable family, he seems to be gaining confidence and branching out a little on his own. He's also much stronger now that he's got steady medication. Tick's got a heart ailment, and before his adoption it nearly did him in a few times."

"That poor boy. I'm so glad he's found a family and a place to belong."

Again the wistfulness in her voice tugged at Silas. He had the urge to put his arm around her. "I met your sister the other night. Is it just you two, or are your parents traveling with you?"

She shook her head and lowered her chin until her hat brim shielded her face. "My parents are both gone now, my father when I was ten and my mother more recently."

"I'm so sorry. I know how that feels. My mother passed away when I was twelve."

When she raised her beautiful gray eyes, they were clear and untroubled. She busied herself folding napkins and stowing things in the basket. "So it's just Francine and me. But the acting troupe is like a family. My parents were both actors, and Francine and I have followed in their footsteps."

"So you've never known another life but the theater?"

"No. It's been my whole life up to now."

Her profile did all sorts of strange things to his concentration. When she turned to look at him, he found himself staring at her pink lips and had to tear his gaze away to focus on what she was saying.

"What do you remember best about your mother?"

"Rocks."

"Rocks?"

"She loved to collect rocks. We'd walk for miles along the lakeshore, and she would pick up rocks. Interesting shapes or colors. We'd take them home and polish them. Sometimes we'd find an agate and break it open. Mother always said collecting rocks reminded her of how temporary we are and how big and powerful God is. Those rocks had been around since creation in one form or another, and here they were on the shore just waiting for us to come along and polish them up. And she could spot the potential, the beauty inside the rock that just needed to be let out. She said rocks were like people. If we let God polish us, He can reveal His good work in us until we can be things of beauty to glorify Him."

"I wondered why you had a handkerchief full of rocks the first time we met."

He grinned. "I still collect rocks, fossils, petrified wood, anything that catches my eye really. You should hear my housekeeper complain about dusting them. They are a nuisance, I suppose, but I like them. Though Sherman knocks them on the floor from time to time when he's put out with me."

"Sherman?"

"My cat. He came with the house. I

named him Sherman because he's as relentless and bossy as a general."

"I'd love to meet him sometime."

"I have a feeling you will. Let's go see what the boys are up to." He took her hand and helped her to her feet.

When they got to the shore, the boys were ready to fish. Willow grimaced as they baited their hooks, and Phin swaggered a bit when he told her it was all right, he'd bait her hook for her since she was a girl.

"What do I do if I actually manage to snag a fish?"

"Holler and we'll come help you." Phin swung her hook over the water and handed her the pole. He scampered away to join the boys upstream.

Once he was out of earshot, she laughed. "He's quite the gallant young man under all that bravado."

"That's Phin. He wants everyone to think he's tough, but there's a heart of butter in there. Watch how he manages the younger boys. They think the world of him. Natural leadership there. I have a feeling he would make a great pastor someday."

"Speaking of pastors, I had no idea until today you were a minister. It's clear you're in the right profession. I've never listened to a more gifted preacher."

Pleasure shot through him at her praise. He shrugged, but he knew he'd pull out her words to treasure again later.

"Did you always want to be a minister?"

"I come from a long line of ministers, and I never really considered doing anything else. I can't imagine not being a pastor."

"Your father must be so proud of you."

He shook his head, his chest pinching. "I hope someday he will be. He's not too pleased at the moment. His plans for me never included a small congregation in Colorado. My father is Dr. Clyburn Hamilton, and he serves as the head of our denomination. According to him, I'm supposed to be teaching in the seminary where he is currently the president, writing theology books, and pastoring a large church in Philadelphia where he would be able to better oversee my advancement within the ranks."

"Why aren't you?"

"That might be right for some pastors, and I know a lot who would jump at the chance, but my calling is to preach and serve in a smaller congregation. My father didn't mind my getting a few years of experience in a church in Kansas City, but he's never approved of my taking this position. In fact, he's sending someone out to review my performance soon, and I have a suspicion if there is the tiniest blemish on that report, he'll see that I'm recalled to Philadelphia before the summer is over."

"He can do that?"

"He's the head of the denomination, and he's determined to bring me to my senses."

Her eyebrows drew together. "It's hard to live up to other people's expectations. Sometimes it's impossible. Opportunities arise, and you realize you have to take them, even if someone else is let down because of them."

"You sound like you speak from experience."

She shrugged. "I have a couple of decisions facing me at the moment."

"Anything I can help with?" He chuckled and covered her hand with his, thrilling at the jolt of pleasure that shot up his arm at the contact. "I'm a pretty good listener."

At that moment the cork float on her line jerked under the water. "What do I do?" She sprang to grab the rod before it landed in the stream.

The boys dropped their poles on the bank and pelted toward them.

Phin reached for her rod, but Silas stopped him. "No, let her do it. Everyone should bring in their first fish by themselves."

"Silas, please." She cast him a pleading glance. "Help me. What do I do?"

"Keep the line tight. Don't let it go slack, or he'll get a run and maybe break it. Keep the tip of the pole up."

The boys all shouted encouragement and advice.

Willow tucked her lower lip in, set her jaw, and braced against the tug of the fish and the current. In no time at all, she'd landed the trout.

"That's a beaut." Phin bent over the fish flopping on the grass. "Biggest trout I've seen."

"Is it?"

"What a whopper. Wait till Dad hears about this." Tick shoved his hair out of his eyes.

The Hebig boys whistled and crowed.

Willow seemed to take this for the applause it was. "What do we do with it now?"

"Take the hook out, put it on the stringer, and peg the line to the bank. Fish for supper."

"Oh no, don't do that." Willow knelt on the grass beside the fish. "The poor thing. I want to let it go."

"What?" Phin jammed his hands on his hips. "After all that work you ain't even gonna eat it?"

Willow cast Silas a pleading glance.

It hurt him to let the fish go — after all, people caught fish to eat them. But he said, "It's her fish. She can do what she wants with it." He lifted the trout and removed the hook. "But you have to let it go yourself. The fisherman in me can't do it."

With a squeamish grimace, she took the slippery animal and leaned over the bank. "There you go, you poor thing. I'm sorry for hauling you out of your home like that."

With a flip and a flicker, the trophy fish disappeared under the rippling water. She rinsed her hands in the stream and wiped them with her handkerchief. "I'm afraid I'll never make a fisherman."

"Just like a girl." Phin grabbed a rock and flicked it at the water where it bounced four times and sank.

"I'll tell you something I am good at though." She picked up another rock and sent it winging over the water. "Seven. Beat that."

The battle was on. They laughed and threw rocks and challenged one another to impossible feats until finally the boys declared they were starving. Willow brought out the turnovers. They ate, licking their fingers and dabbing at the crumbs, not wanting to waste a bite.

Silas leaned back on his palms and stretched his legs out. "You boys can play for another half hour or so. Then we need to head back."

As they bounded away, Willow shook her head. "You're very good with them."

"I was just thinking the same about you." And more. All afternoon he'd been captivated by her. Everything about her pleased him, and he could see her as the mistress of his home and his helpmeet in the church. He could envision her directing the Christmas play and organizing a children's choir. Better yet, he could see her opening his home to hospitality and welcoming him in after a long day at the church.

Silas leaned closer to her and lowered his head. His heart knocked against his ribs, and his palms sweat. He had a feeling his future happiness rested squarely on her answer to his question. "Willow, is there someone I should speak to about courting you? Someone I should ask?"

Her mouth opened, but nothing came out.

He wasn't worried though. The light that had come into her eyes — a look of wonder, hope, expectancy — was answer enough. He threaded his fingers through hers and pressed their palms together.

She found her voice. "There's no one you

have to ask but me." She swallowed, pink coming to tinge her cheeks.

"And?"

"I'd like nothing more."

When they returned to the church, Silas introduced Willow to a waiting Sam Mackenzie, a handsome, easygoing man who put his arms around each of his sons while he thanked Silas for taking them for the afternoon. Mr. Hebig shook Silas's hand and gave Willow a quizzical look and bustled his boys into the wagon for the ride home.

"Let me drop this stuff off at the house. Then I'll walk you home." Silas lifted the bundle of fishing poles and the bait bucket.

"I'll take the basket and the blanket."

They rounded the church to the parsonage. "Just through here. Estelle doesn't work on Sundays, so there's no one here but Sherman." He set the poles on the porch and reached for her burdens. "I'd love to invite you in, but . . ."

"I understand." How nice to have someone so concerned with her reputation.

The minute Silas opened the door, an enormous cat stepped out, wound around his legs for a moment, and regarded her with brilliant green eyes. "This is Sherman. Now you be nice, cat, or you'll be sleeping

117

outside tonight." He ducked into the house to put away the picnic paraphernalia.

Willow sank to the stairs. "Hello, Sherman. My, but you're a handsome fellow in your evening dress."

The animal tilted his head, listening to her, before approaching with his tail held high. She rubbed his cheek, and he butted his head against her hand and let loose a deep purr. Without fear, he climbed into her lap, lay down, and turned over, exposing his white belly for her to rub.

"I've never seen him do that before." Silas leaned against the doorframe and crossed his arms. "What a mush." He'd donned his suit coat and tie and smoothed his hair.

"He's just a big baby, aren't you?" She stroked his soft fur, and he wriggled with pleasure. "I've never had a pet before. We moved around too much. One of the actors in the troupe had a parrot once, but it bit and said naughty words, so my mother made me keep away from it. Sherman seems like a friendly fellow."

"He's usually content to rub against someone's leg, but he never lets a stranger pet him like that. I guess he's got good taste." Silas bent and rubbed Sherman under the chin. "Come on, you silly cat. I've got to get her home."

Walking to the hotel on Silas's arm felt so right, Willow didn't want the trip to end, but her stomach tightened as they approached the theater. What had she done agreeing to Silas's courting her? The offer from New York and all that hung upon her acceptance of it dragged at her like a ball and chain. The company was counting on her to get them to New York City, so much so that they were already making plans, assuming she'd said yes. Only Clement knew she'd asked for time to consider. "You don't have to walk me in. My sister will be waiting for me. She was going to run lines with Philip late this afternoon, and I was supposed to join them."

"Nonsense. I'd like to see where you work, and I'd like to meet your sister again."

Apprehension feathered across Willow's skin as she let them in through the side stage door. Though she knew Francine would eventually need to know about Silas, Willow was loathe to reveal their relationship so soon. What she felt for Silas — feelings that were growing every day — was private. And his desire to court her was so new and fresh that she feared laying herself open to her sister's criticism or judgment would somehow tarnish it. "We can peek in and see if they're here. If not, she'll be at the hotel." They walked down the narrow hallway full of doors. "This is my dressing room. Well, Francine's and mine. We share."

Passing into the wings, Francine's voice came to them, and Willow's heart sank. "Where has Willow been all day? When she left, she said she was going to church of all places. I don't know where she gets these odd notions."

Footsteps tapped on the stage floor, and heat rushed up Willow's cheeks. She called out before Francine could say anything else to embarrass both of them. "Is anyone here?"

"You're certainly late enough. Do you have someone with you?"

"I'm sorry for being late, though there was no set time for this rehearsal," Willow gently reminded Francine. "And yes, I've brought someone with me." Half the lanterns along the footboards had been lit, casting odd shadows on the painted backdrop depicting Ferndean Manor. "This is Silas Hamilton. You met him earlier this week. Silas, my sister, Francine Starr, and this is Philip Moncrieff."

Francine's eyes glittered. "So that's where you've been disappearing to. I might've known it. Meeting a man on the sly."

Philip rubbed his chin and leered. "Hmm,

you've got some unsuspected depths, my dear."

Willow's back stiffened. "This is the *Reverend* Silas Hamilton. He pastors a church here in Martin City."

The transformation from petulant to flirtatious happened in an instant. Francine's eyelashes fluttered, her mouth went into a pout, and she held out her hand. "My, my, Reverend Hamilton. It is a pleasure to see you again. Willow tends to wander off at every opportunity, and I do worry about her. I had no idea she was in your company."

Silas took her hand briefly. "Miss Starr, Willow was kind enough to help me this afternoon. I had five small charges eager for a picnic. She accompanied me, helping me keep them entertained."

"You must call me Francine." She folded her hands at her waist and raked her gaze over Willow. "An afternoon shepherding children at a picnic explains Willow's windblown and disheveled appearance."

Instinctively, Willow's hands started up to smooth her hair, but she forced herself to lower her arms and stand still. It wouldn't matter anyway. The damage had been done. How many times had first her mother then Francine drilled it into her that she must

121

appear professional at all times in public? It was her duty as an actress to preserve the illusion of perfection, lest the patrons of the theater decide she was a mere mortal, breaking the spell and thus the desire to believe in the performance.

"Willow always looks charming." Silas sent her a smile, his eyes seeming to drink in her face.

Philip strolled over to Willow's other side, standing way too close, nearly gagging her with the cloying scent of hair oil and cloves.

Silas squeezed Willow's elbow and guided her closer to his side. "Miss Starr — Francine — I'd like to invite you and Willow to dinner at the hotel tonight. I would enjoy getting to know you better." He turned to Philip. "You're invited as well, of course."

"Oh, he hasn't the time, since he's supposed to be blocking a scene with Clement in just a little while, but I'd be delighted to take supper with you." Francine edged between Willow and Silas, taking his arm and not bothering to look at Willow. "Thank you for looking after my little sister this afternoon. I'm sure she and the boys had a nice time on that picnic. It's so rare she gets to spend time with children her own age." She led him away, and Silas cast a helpless glance over his shoulder to Willow.

Willow ground her teeth. Just like Francine to put her in her place, relegating her to the rank of child who needed to be watched. She followed them, and Philip fell into step with her.

Philip's laugh slid over her like axle grease, thick and black, and he lowered his voice. "I thought there was something different about you lately. You've got even more of a dreamy-eyed look than usual. I suspect yonder swain is the cause? A preacher? How quaint. But don't expect Francine to take it lying down."

Willow said nothing and kept walking.

He leaned closer. "I always suspected your still waters ran deep." He reached for her hand, and she flinched. "A little seasoning will be the making of you, get you ready for New York." He laughed again and turned in at his dressing room.

"Willow? Are you all right?" Silas turned at the stage door to wait for her.

She straightened. "Of course."

Silas frowned. "Was that man pestering you?"

"Philip was just being Philip. It's nothing to worry about."

"Come along, Willow." Francine crossed her arms. "Stop dawdling with Philip. You've still got to clean up and change. I'm not going to be seen in public with you looking like that. While you're doing that, I'll freshen up as well."

Willow kept her chin high and refused to let her hurt or embarrassment show. One would think she would be used to the constant criticism, but somehow having it happen in front of Silas made it so much worse.

EIGHT

Willow battled the diving swallows in her middle as she made her way downstairs to the hotel foyer, smoothing the skirts of her pale pink dress and fingering her single strand of pearls.

Francine came behind her, wearing the diamonds and an elaborate evening gown that showed off her tiny waist and curving bosom.

Silas met them at the foot of the stairs and led them to the dining room.

The restaurant, lavishly appointed with chandeliers, crystal, china, and pristine linens, buzzed with conversation. Discrete waiters threaded through tables with laden trays.

"You look beautiful. That's a very becoming dress." Silas's look was appreciative and just a hint possessive, sending a thrill through her. He bent to whisper in her ear as he held her chair. "And I'm not just saying that. You take my breath away." He hadn't even looked at Francine.

"Men, aren't they funny?" Francine smoothed her bodice and opened her fan. "Of course you wouldn't know that dress is not exactly the latest fashion, but Willow insisted on wearing it tonight. I try my best, but . . ." She spread her hands as if she couldn't possibly be blamed for any of Willow's shortcomings.

The confidence his compliment had given her drained from Willow like an audience leaving a theater.

A waiter handed them each an enormous handwritten menu in a leather cover.

"Hmm." Francine sniffed, though she'd eaten in this same dining room daily and knew every dish on the menu. "I suppose this establishment isn't terrible, but when I think of some of the fine restaurants I've dined in . . . Have you ever been to New York, Reverend Hamilton?"

"Please, call me Silas, and yes, I've been to New York several times."

"Really? I'm quite impressed. So far, I haven't found a really well-traveled male in Martin City. Are you perhaps from somewhere back East?"

"Ohio originally. On Lake Erie. More recently my family hails from Philadelphia."

Silas smiled at Willow, sharing a private moment of remembrance. He didn't seem inclined to open up to Francine about his father the way he had to Willow, and she cherished his trust in her.

Francine spent the meal being charming and carefully edging Willow out of the conversation. Silas proved adept at including her, and when his hand came under the tablecloth to clasp hers, she wanted to laugh. He had caught on quickly to Francine's ways and didn't seem inclined to be blinded by her charm.

The waiter poured their after-dinner coffee. Would Silas tell Francine he was now courting Willow, or did he think Willow should be the one to share that information?

"Why, hello, Reverend Hamilton. I didn't expect to see you here tonight." A matronly woman Willow recognized from church that morning — she'd taken considerable time greeting Silas after the service — stopped by their table. A man and younger woman — a daughter? — stood behind her.

Silas rose, placing his napkin on the table. Though he smiled at the newcomer, Willow had the feeling it was forced. "Mrs. Drabble, good evening. Have you met the Starrs?"

The woman's eyebrows rose until they

nearly collided with her hairline. "I haven't had the pleasure." An edge to her voice caused Willow to doubt any pleasure the woman might be claiming.

Silas let his hand rest on Willow's shoulder in a possessive gesture. "Have you had a chance to attend the theater? Willow is truly amazing as Jane Eyre, and Francine will delight you in her role as well. Willow, Francine, this is Mr. and Mrs. Drabble and their daughter, Alicia."

Mrs. Drabble's upper lip twitched like she'd just smelled sour milk. "Of course I haven't been to the theater. A young man asked only a few days ago if he could take Alicia to the theater. He left with no doubt as to my feelings on the subject of such idle entertainment. I'm shocked you admit to attending."

Willow knew that look and that tone. There were some who felt female entertainers were synonymous with fallen women, that they did more than sing, dance, or act for a living. Her cheeks reddened, but she held her composure.

Francine rolled her eyes and seemed to be sizing up the other woman. If it came to a war of words or worse, Willow's money was on Francine to win.

A bemused smile took hold of Silas. "Why

should it surprise you that I would enjoy an evening's entertainment and culture? I enjoy a good thespian endeavor as much as the next man, minister or not. I'm expecting to attend several more times before this play has finished its run here in Martin City."

Mrs. Drabble gaped, not unlike the trout Willow had landed earlier that day. The resemblance caused a giggle to shoot out of her, and she tried to disguise it as a cough. From the stormy look the woman shot at her, Willow had to assume she'd failed.

Her eye caught that of the young, blond woman beside Mrs. Drabble, and she nearly giggled again at the mischievous light there. Something about Alicia Drabble appealed to Willow, and she thought they could easily be friends.

Mr. Drabble checked his watch. "I think it's time to go, dear."

When he had led his wife away, Willow relaxed.

Francine sipped from her cup. "A member of your congregation, I take it?"

"Yes, he serves as an elder and she as a deaconess."

Willow swallowed. Silas didn't seem at all worried about how his courting her might affect his church, and he knew them better than she did, but she couldn't help the uneasy feelings coursing through her.

Francine placed her napkin on the table. "Thank you for a nice evening, Mr. Hamilton, but Willow and I should be going. We need our beauty sleep after all."

Silas pulled out her chair then Willow's and walked them to the base of the stairs. He held on to Willow's arm, letting Francine go up first. "I hope you have pleasant dreams. I'll call on you soon." His fingers squeezed her arm, and he took his leave.

Once in the hotel room, Francine eyed Willow. "You surprise me. Playing paddy fingers with the local preacher? Still, I guess you've found a way to amuse yourself for the next few weeks before we go to New York."

Willow unclasped her necklace and laid the pearls in their velvet box. She moistened her lips and swallowed, staring into the mirror on the dressing table.

"You are just amusing yourself, right?" Francine marched over and grabbed Willow's shoulder, turning her around. "Dally all you want, but don't let it go to your head. The entire company is counting on you. You heard Clement. Without you, there will be no New York City. If I thought for a minute you were serious about Silas Hamilton . . ." She searched Willow's face, then tipped her head back and laughed. "Of course you aren't. Nobody would turn down New York for a backwater preacher, no matter how handsome he is."

A week after his dinner at the hotel, Silas drew his chair up to the Drabble table. Time for pouring a little oil on the water.

"I'm so glad you could make time to visit. You've been so busy. Why, I even stopped by the parsonage twice in the evening this week only to find it dark." Mrs. Drabble set the last serving dish on the table and took her place across from Silas.

Walter Drabble bowed his head, mumbled a few words of prayer, and grabbed the soup tureen.

Alicia sat next to her mother, as pretty as always, but she reminded Silas of a porcelain doll, closed off and aloof. He knew it wasn't fair to compare her to the vibrant, glowing Willow, but he couldn't seem to help himself. Where Willow experienced life around her, Alicia seemed merely to observe. And yet, he chided himself. Perhaps Alicia was only unresponsive to him, as he was to her. Perhaps if she truly came to care for someone, she would come alive to that man, and he would see her as Silas saw Willow.

You're getting fanciful. You're seeing the

world all rainbows and music. And all because of Willow.

"Aren't you hungry, Reverend Hamilton?" Beatrice held out the plate of roast beef, inviting him to take a portion.

"Oh yes. I'm sorry. It smells wonderful."

"Alicia made it." Beatrice beamed. "She's such a good cook, and she took such pains when she knew she was preparing dinner for you."

Alicia closed her eyes for a moment and took a slow breath. She picked at her food, rolling the creamed peas and onions on her plate with the tines of her fork.

Mrs. Drabble smoothed her hair toward the coil on the back of her neck — hair so black it must surely owe its jetty tones to artifice? "You didn't say where you were during the evenings this past week. Has someone fallen ill? Are you visiting parishioners?"

Silas finished chewing the tender roast and swallowed. "The members of the church seem to be in remarkably good health. I haven't had much visitation, and I've accomplished much of that during the day. I find evening visitation of the sick to be too disruptive to the household."

"I see. But if you weren't visiting, where have you gotten to at night?" Beatrice fixed him with a stare that said she wasn't going to give up until she knew his whereabouts.

"Actually, I've been enjoying the theater this week." Willow had left tickets for him at the office for any night he could come, and both times he could make it, he'd taken Willow out afterward to the hotel restaurant for coffee and long talks. He was already plotting when he could free his schedule up to see her again. If it wasn't for Mrs. Drabble's insistence and his twinges of guilt at avoiding her, he would be in the front row of the theater right now.

Mrs. Drabble sniffed. "Reverend Hamilton, you're young, so I'm sure you will appreciate the guidance of those with a bit more experience of life than you. I think, as someone who feels, well, a certain motherly regard toward you" — she cast a fond glance at Alicia then back to Silas — "I think I must caution you against your current actions. The theater isn't the best place for a pastor to be seen. As to socializing with those actors and actresses . . ." She stopped, shook her head as if any imbecile should know the dangers, and continued. "It casts a rather bad light on the church. You know as a pastor you are called upon to represent the church in the community. To have you frequenting that establishment and fraternizing with those people besmirches our reputation."

Silas held on to his temper. "Mrs. Drabble, I assure you there is nothing objectionable in the play, and the cast members are fine, upstanding people. Perhaps if you came to see the performance and spent some time with the actors, you'd see there's no harm in it. Several of the congregation have attended the play."

"You're leading them astray with such an attitude. They are partaking in questionable entertainment only because of your example." Her mouth puckered like she'd bitten into a green apple. "You act as if there is nothing wrong with such entertainment or the people who purvey it."

"That's because I do believe there is nothing wrong with it or the people. I would encourage the members of the church to see the play. It will edify and enrich, broaden their perspectives, challenge their minds, and give them much enjoyment, not to mention the interaction with others in the community." His voice had risen, and he strove to modulate his tone.

Walter ignored the conversation, shoveling food into his mouth and keeping his eyes on his plate. Alicia's eyes flicked to the clock on the wall behind Silas every few seconds as if willing the evening to be over soon.

"As to the people, I find them delightful."
Especially Willow.

Mrs. Drabble put on her most patient face.

Silas gritted his teeth and took a firm hold on his tongue. Mrs. Drabble being annoying and opinionated was hard to deal with, but Mrs. Drabble being patient and instructive was worse. Much worse.

"I only caution you because I care. I understand what it is like to be young and to have your head turned by someone unsuitable." Here her glance shifted to take in Alicia, and she frowned. "It's hard to be objective when feelings become entangled. One might get the wrong idea if you were to keep company with one of those actresses I saw you dining with."

"Mrs. Drabble, thank you for your concern, but —"

"Now, hear me out. One must be so careful when one is in a position of leadership. If you were to become . . . entangled with an actress, even only in rumor, it would damage your reputation. Someone might get the idea you were actually courting one of those girls with the idea of marrying her. The person you marry must be suitable not only to your personality but to your position. After all, Caesar's wife must be above reproach, and bright is the light that shines upon the throne . . . or in this case, the pulpit."

He inhaled deeply and set his fork on his plate. "Mrs. Drabble —"

"Now, I know it's hard, but if you'll just listen to reason, there are plenty of nice girls in the church. As you know, I've cherished the notion that you might find Alicia more than pleasing. She would make a lovely minister's wife. She has a spotless reputation — I've seen to that. She can cook and clean and sew, and she's excellent with children and organization. And I'm sure you would agree she's more than passably pretty."

Silas pushed his chair back.

Alicia stepped in before he could say something. "Mother, that is enough." She rounded on Silas. "Why don't you tell her to keep her nose out of your business? Mother, I have no intention of marrying Silas Hamilton or anyone else you might try to push me at. Silas must be weary of it, and I know I certainly am."

Beatrice reacted as if she'd sat on a branding iron. She jumped up, threw her napkin on the table, and plonked her fists on her hips. "Young lady, don't you take that tone with me, especially not in front of a guest. You don't know what's best for you. I do. Now apologize to the reverend and sit down."

Alicia returned to her seat, but her eyes glittered with rebellion. "I do apologize to the reverend. Silas, I'm sorry for the way my mother tries to manipulate you. I'm sorry she's plotted our marriage when it's plain we are unsuited for one another. You've been patient and gallant. Too patient perhaps. I could tell the moment I saw you with Willow Starr you had great feelings for her. I only hope she returns those feelings for you. You deserve to be happy."

Mrs. Drabble sank to her chair, her mouth slack.

Silas was sure her daughter had never spoken so boldly against her mother. He admired her grit. Not too many folks had the fortitude to take on such a determined woman.

"Is it true? You have feelings for an actress?"

"That's right, Mrs. Drabble. I'm courting Willow Starr."

The shock vanished from her face, replaced by anger. "The board is going to hear about this. Can you imagine what the district supervisor will say when he hears?

Not to mention what your father will say."

The threat in her voice tightened Silas's neck muscles. What would his father say about Willow? He folded his napkin. "I think it is time for me to go. I'm sorry you feel Willow Starr isn't right for me, but I am a grown man and able to make my own choice. I'm sure that when you get to know her, you'll recognize what a special young woman she is. I do hope you'll do your best to welcome her into the congregation."

As he walked up the hill to the church, he couldn't help but feel proud of Alicia for finally standing up to her mother. At least that was one problem off his plate. No more trying to find a tactful way of evading Mrs. Drabble's matchmaking plans. And probably no more escaping her invitations to dinner. He doubted he'd be invited back anytime soon.

As to what his father would say . . . He sighed. It had been such a long time since he'd pleased his father in any way. Their communications tended to be formal, stilted, and on his father's side at least, loaded with long-suffering patience as he waited for his son to get his ridiculous notions out of his system and return to the life mapped out for him since birth. Silas was sure Willow Starr factored nowhere in his father's plans.

But clearing the air with Mrs. Drabble had assured Silas of one thing. He knew without a doubt his heart belonged to Willow. He was in love, and he couldn't wait to find just the right way to tell her.

NINE

A busy week followed his dinner at the Drabbles, and he found himself unable to spend much time with Willow after all. Mrs. Drabble sent word she would be unable to help with the orphanage. He knew he should go see her and try to smooth out the rift between them, but he kept putting it off.

Sunday morning, Mrs. Drabble was absent from church, though Alicia and Mr. Drabble attended. He tried to speak to Walter Drabble before they left but got waylaid by the Mackenzies and an invitation to lunch. Mr. Drabble slipped out, taking Alicia with him.

Willow came to church, edging into the back at the last minute, and at the Mackenzies' insistence was included in the lunch invitation. The meal and the company were excellent and encouraged Silas. Willow was especially taken with the baby, and something about seeing her holding an infant, so enraptured, made Silas's insides turn to porridge.

Monday evening, Silas found himself yawning right after supper. "Sherman, if I didn't have these church records to catch up on, I'd fall right into bed."

Sherman seemed unconcerned, continuing to wash his snowy paws.

Another yawn overtook Silas, and he scrubbed his hair, stretching and trying to wake up. He hadn't been sleeping too well. Thoughts of Willow kept him awake. And the issue of the ill feelings between himself and the Drabbles. He was also worried about Kenneth Hayes. Since their talk, Kenneth had missed several Sundays in a row at church. "Tomorrow I need to go see him."

If Kenneth had made his intentions known to the girl's father and been rejected, it might explain his absence, but if he'd put off asking permission and didn't want to face Silas, that might also prompt him to avoid church. And there might be another reason altogether. No matter. It deserved investigation.

A knock sounded on the door, and Silas levered himself up from his desk. He hoped whoever it was wouldn't want to stay long, and he squashed that inhospitable thought before it could take root. If someone needed him, he was there to serve.

Jesse Mackenzie stood on the porch, his face like a thundercloud.

"Evening, Jesse. What's wrong? Is it Matilda? Or one of the grandkids?"

"No, no, nothing like that. The board has called a special meeting over at the church." He shoved his hands into his pockets and rocked on his heels.

Silas blinked and reached for the doorjamb. "A special meeting? Tonight? What for?"

"Mrs. Drabble called it. Well, I suppose officially Walter Drabble called it, but she's pulling the strings, same as always. Says he's got something important that needs to be discussed."

Silas reached for his suit coat and tried to tamp down his ruffled hair. "Is everyone there?"

"Yep, the whole board, elders and deacons and the two deaconesses. Mrs. Drabble seems to have made a good recovery from whatever kept her away from church yesterday." Jesse paced the porch. "She won't say why she called the meeting, just insisted everyone attend, especially you."

A knot formed between Silas's shoulder

blades as he shrugged into his coat, but he cautioned himself against giving in to dread and despair. If only he hadn't put off going to see her. These kinds of problems never got solved by ignoring them. "Maybe something to do with the orphanage again. The open house is set for next week." A weak hope, but something to grasp on to.

Jesse shrugged and continued to pace the porch floor while Silas doused the lamps and closed the door.

Lights blazed from the church windows, and Silas paused on the top step to appreciate what a pretty picture the white-steepled building made with all the colored glass windows.

When they entered the building, the tension in the room bombarded him. Five people stared back at him, six if you included Jesse. Two elders, two deacons, and two deaconesses. Matilda wore a worried look but smiled encouragingly, while the Drabbles looked grim. Mrs. Drabble in particular looked as if she were sharpening her verbal knives. The other two, Larry Horton, a deacon, and Ned Meeker, an elder, had separated into their usual seats. Larry sat with the Drabbles, and Meeker just behind Matilda. Jesse strode up the aisle and took a seat next to his wife.

"Good evening." Silas walked up the aisle and turned to face them. "I'm afraid you have me at a disadvantage. I don't know why this meeting has been called. Does it have something to do with the orphanage?" He searched Matilda Mackenzie's face, but she shook her head and gave a slight shrug. Clearly she'd been kept in the dark as well.

Mrs. Drabble poked her husband in the ribs. "Go ahead."

Walter took his time unfolding himself from his seat. "Silas —"

"Reverend!" Mrs. Drabble hissed the word, poking him again.

Walter began again. "Reverend, it has come to the attention of the board that you may be . . . socializing with an undesirable element. Some of the board members feel you shouldn't do this." He sat down again and folded his arms across his chest.

"An undesirable element?" Silas's heart began to thud, and his ribs squeezed tight.

Mrs. Drabble leaned forward and grasped the back of the pew in front of her. "Don't pretend you don't know. You told me with your own mouth you were courting an *actress*." Her eyes glowed like coals, and hectic color stained her cheeks. "It's unseemly, and it's got to stop."

Silas braced his palms on the railing that

divided the platform from the pews. "You called a board meeting to discuss my private business?" He kept his voice even, but his fingers bit into the banister.

Her chin went up. "You have no one to blame but yourself. I tried to follow the biblical procedure. I tried to talk to you about this privately in my home, but you wouldn't listen. Now I have no choice but to bring it before the board."

Jesse leaned forward. "Is this about Willow?"

"Exactly." Mrs. Drabble snapped off the word like a breaking a twig. "And what kind of outlandish name is Willow anyway? It's probably not her real name at all. All these actor-types use fake names. It's like lying."

Every time she spoke, Larry Horton nodded, and Silas had the feeling she'd been over it all with him already. He seemed firmly in her camp.

Larry squinted. "I can't believe this even needs to be brought up. Everybody knows women entertainers are of low character. You might's well have paraded up Main Street with one of the working girls from the Lead Pig Saloon on your arm as bring that actress to church."

Silas's head snapped back. "That is a scurrilous remark if I ever heard one. You're making generalities and assumptions that could have serious consequences. Rumors like that do a lot of damage, and I take exception to you speaking that way about the woman I'm courting."

Jesse nodded. "Have you even met this girl, Larry? Do you know her? I have. She's been a guest in my home. She's as lovely and charming and as good as your own daughters. I'd stake my silver mine on it." His mighty fist slammed down on the rail before him. "She's an actress, and a very good one, I might add, and nothing in her behavior indicated she had anything in common with a saloon girl. As far as I'm concerned, she's welcome in my home and in this church."

Larry's neck grew mottled with red splotches. "We're not talking about your home, and she's certainly welcome to attend church and change her ways. What we are talking about is Silas keeping company with a woman of poor reputation and compromising the work of the church and the very Gospel he proclaims."

Matilda cleared her throat. "Larry, those are some very strong words. As Jesse has said, we've attended the play being performed, and we've had Willow in our home, not to mention meeting her at a reception in the hotel where her manners and behavior were exemplary. She's done nothing and said nothing to indicate she is of low moral character. In fact, it is just the opposite. She speaks of her faith naturally and openly. You mentioned her reputation, but reputation is something manufactured by others. Reputation has nothing to do with character, and everything I've witnessed tells me her character is very good."

Ned Meeker raised his hand. His pale eyes looked out of a face as wrinkled as crumpled paper. He had years of wisdom, experience, and leadership to draw on, and Silas had always found him a good advisor. "Folks, how many of us here have met the young lady in question?"

The Mackenzies raised their hands.

Mrs. Drabble did as well. "I met her at the hotel restaurant where our pastor was dining with her and her sister. Bold as anything."

Ned pursed his lips. "Have you spoken to her beyond saying hello?"

Silas cast back to that evening and realized Beatrice hadn't even acknowledged the Starrs beyond a scowl or two.

"Well no, not to say spoken to. But I'm no fool. I know what I know."

Ned eased himself to his feet, his knees

cracking. "Folks, this whole meeting leaves a rather bad taste in my mouth." His gnarled hands grasped the pew ahead of him, and his breath wheezed, testament to years spent in mine shafts and rock dust. "Pastor Hamilton has never given us cause to doubt his judgment. If he says Miss Starr is a fitting companion, then that's good enough for me. There's them that talks about being good and aren't, and them that are good and find themselves talked about." His gaze rested heavily on each one there before he eased back down onto the pew and rested his hands in his lap.

Matilda turned and patted his hand.

Silas decided it was time for him to step in. "I thank you, Ned, for your support, and you too, Jesse and Matilda. I think the crux of the matter here is that there have been opinions formed without knowing the facts. Perhaps if you were to get to know Willow, you'd all come to see what I've seen." He looked sternly at the Drabble contingent. "All I'm asking is that you give Willow a chance. Get to know her and the other folks at the theater. I'm not saying they're all saints, but Willow is a fine young woman, and I intend to marry her."

Mrs. Drabble sucked in a gasp and coughed. "Marriage?"

Silas frowned. "Mrs. Drabble, surely you didn't think I would court a woman if I didn't think she was suitable for marriage?"

She fanned herself with her handkerchief. "You mean you would refuse my daughter and all the other nice church girls in favor of an *actress?*"

"Mrs. Drabble, I don't think a church board meeting is the place to discuss this. Alicia and I have made our feelings clear to you on this matter. She has no more interest in marrying me than I have in marrying her."

Larry stood and creased the crown of his hat, his jaw set like granite and a flinty look in his eye. "Looks to me that even if we was to vote, we'd be split, just like usual, and the pastor would break the tie in favor of himself. But I warn you, if you bring that woman into the parsonage, you'll find more than a few families in this church unhappy about it. Not to mention the denomination. I haven't turned in my questionnaire yet, and neither have a few others. If you insist on cramming this woman down our throats, you might find yourself on the outside of this church looking in."

He jammed his hat onto his head and stalked out. Mr. and Mrs. Drabble followed after him, leaving Ned and the Mackenzies.

Silas sank onto the front pew and put his face into his hands. He'd been blithely following his heart while a chasm opened between his feet and split the church board right down the middle. He had underestimated Mrs. Drabble's vitriol. Larry's words both surprised him and hurt him, since he'd never borne any ill will toward the man and had assumed they were not only friends but had a mutual respect for one another.

Jesse squeezed Silas's shoulder. "I'm sorry, Silas. I had no idea this was coming, or I'd have tried to head them off somehow."

He raised his head to look at Jesse, Ned, and Matilda. "What should I do about this?"

Ned pursed his lips and rubbed his hand down his cheek. "For now, nothing. Best to let us try to talk to them. They're so worked up, I have a feeling anything you tried to do would be taken wrong."

Matilda threaded her reticule over her wrist. "What about the supervisor's visit? We really should try to get this resolved before his arrival. A church board with daggers drawn wouldn't be the best endorsement for our pastor's leadership abilities."

Silas shuddered, imagining what his father would say. *I told you not to take that church. You've failed. Failed me. Failed the denomination. Failed God.*

"Now Matilda, don't tease like that. You've made Silas go white as a winter moon." Jesse whacked him on the shoulder. "I'm sure we can get this thing turned around before it comes to that. You're a fine pastor, and you're not doing anything wrong. The church will see that, and Beatrice will, too, once she gets over her peeve at you not marrying Alicia."

"I hope you're right. I just know if people will give Willow a chance, they'll come to love her like I do."

"Leave it to us. We'll see what we can do." Jesse helped Matilda to her feet.

Early Tuesday afternoon Willow slipped from the theater in search of solitude and a place to think. Philip had been particularly obnoxious today, standing too close, whispering crass comments and suggestions until she wanted to slap his face. He'd gotten worse ever since he'd learned Willow was seeing Silas, as if her being in a relationship with a man meant she was open to much more.

The early morning showers had given way, and the world reminded her of a freshly scrubbed child, rosy and warm. She lifted her face to the sunshine, letting it warm her through, trying to forget for a moment the expectations and responsibilities of the theater, especially those of Philip and Francine. And yet no amount of fresh air and sunshine could lift that weight.

What was she going to do? Clement was pushing for her to sign the contract, Francine had already started planning her new wardrobe for a New York fall season, and more than one of the cast and crew had congratulated Willow on her success and commented on how they were looking forward to the big city.

And every moment she spent with Silas, every long walk, every time he held her hand, every time he caressed her face, bound her more and more to him and his future here. How could she choose? How could she follow her heart and stay when her head said she had to go?

Downstream the trees grew closer to the water, and Willow had to duck under their branches. The game path she followed beckoned her to continue, and she wended her way along Martin Creek farther than she'd ventured on previous rambles.

Around a bend, the trees opened on a little glade with a cabin in the center. As she stood undecided whether to go on or turn back, a movement caught her eye.

The door opened, and a man and woman

emerged. The woman threw herself into the man's arms, and he kissed her again.

Willow realized she was intruding on a private moment, and she turned to hurry away. Her foot landed on a twig, snapping it like a rifle shot. The couple broke apart, and Willow froze.

She knew them. Or the girl, at least. Though she was disheveled, Willow recognized the girl she'd seen in the hotel restaurant with Mrs. Drabble. This had to be Alicia. Silas had mentioned in passing that Mrs. Drabble recently had hopes of his marrying her daughter, but that they weren't at all suited. And here she was alone with a man in an isolated cabin. Tears streamed down her cheeks, and her shoulders shook.

"Are you all right? Do you need help?" She didn't want to intrude, but neither did she want to leave the girl if she truly was distressed. Willow took the measure of the man still standing in the doorway holding Alicia's hand, but he seemed to pose no threat to her or Alicia.

Regardless, they shouldn't be here alone together, and the guilty looks on their faces said they knew it.

Alicia held out her hand. "Please, don't go."

The man frowned. "What are you doing?"

"We can't go on like this. I have to talk to someone —" She broke off on a sob.

The man shoved his hands in his pockets and stared at the ground.

Willow walked up the slope slowly. "You're Mrs. Drabble's daughter, right? Alicia?"

"Yes." The girl hung her head.

Knowing she must choose her words carefully, Willow clasped her hands at her waist. "Are you in some kind of trouble?" Stepping close to Alicia, she lowered her voice. "Does your mother know where you are?"

"No, and she can't know." Alicia grabbed Willow's arm. "Please, promise me you won't tell her, and please, please, don't tell Silas." Tears flowed down the girl's cheeks, and she bit her lower lip. Dropping her clasp on Willow's wrist, she turned and threw herself into the man's arms, sobbing on his shoulder.

He held her tenderly, his face a mask of misery and tenderness. "You're that actress, Willow Starr, aren't you?" He spoke across the top of Alicia's head.

"Yes, I'm Willow Star." She eyed the young man and leaned a bit to the side to see into the cabin. A table and two rough chairs, a cold fireplace, and a bed in the corner with the blanket hanging half off comprised the furnishings.

"My name's Kenneth Hayes. All I did was kiss her, I promise. Nothing else happened."

Willow pressed her fingertips to her brow and squeezed her eyes shut, trying to think. Alicia's sobs made it difficult. She wanted to believe them. What should she say? What should she do? What would Silas do in this situation?

Opening her eyes, she decided to take charge. Clearly neither of these two was capable at the moment. "Alicia, stop crying and come down to the stream with me. We'll wash your face, and you can try to get a hold of yourself." She motioned for Kenneth to stay behind. "We'll be back."

Alicia sniffed and nodded, following Willow like a child.

When they reached the stream, Willow handed her a handkerchief. "Wash, and we'll talk."

"You won't tell my mother, will you? Or Silas?"

"I won't make a promise I can't keep, Alicia, and I won't lie. You know meeting a man alone like this is wrong. If anyone came to find out, you'd be ruined. Who is Kenneth Hayes anyway?"

"He's the man I love more than anything in the world. And he loves me." She dabbed at her red-rimmed eyes and blotchy, damp cheeks. "I've loved him since the moment I first met him."

Willow kept her voice neutral. "You realize you're compromising your reputation by meeting him here? And you're putting yourself in a situation where things could quickly get out of hand and overwhelm you. You might find yourself, in the heat of the moment, doing something you'd later regret."

Alicia wadded the handkerchief into her fist. "I know, but what can we do? I knew my mother would never let me marry Kenneth, and he even went to Silas for advice. Silas said it was Kenneth's duty to ask permission to call on me, that sneaking around was wrong." A hiccup jarred her. "So he did. He asked permission, and they refused. Mother wouldn't hear tell of my marrying a mere miner. And Father does whatever Mother says. She threatened to lock me in my room or send me away to my aunt's. And she forbad me ever to see Kenneth again."

"I'm sorry, Alicia, but is sneaking around the best choice here?"

"It's the *only* choice. What would you do if you couldn't be with the man you love?" Her chin lifted, challenging Willow to walk in her shoes for a while.

Her heart broke for the couple. What an untenable position. If she had to stop seeing Silas, it would break her. She couldn't imagine her life without him. The power of her love for him overwhelmed her, changed how she saw the world, how she saw herself. In that moment, indecision fell away, and her future crystallized. She was willing and ready to give up her career and everything it offered the minute he asked her to. Her future was here, with Silas.

"I don't know what to tell you, but I do know you have to stop seeing each other in secret. Meeting together like this, away from everyone, with your feelings so strong, eventually your emotions are going to get the better of you, and you'll cross a line you can't get back over ever again. Please, go to Silas together and ask him what you should do. He'll help you. He can talk to your parents."

"He can't. My mother is so angry with him right now I don't know what she would do if he showed up at her house. After his last dinner at our place, she wouldn't take a diamond-studded suggestion from him. I've never seen her so angry. Then there was the board meeting. If she was angry before, she was white hot afterward."

"What happened?"

"When Silas came over for dinner, we both made it clear to Mother that marriage to each other was out of the question. Mother already knew I was in love with Kenneth, and Silas all but declared his love for you. She really let him have it, about how you weren't a suitable candidate for a pastor's wife and how he owed it to his congregation to choose someone who was above reproach. She's very class conscious, and she thinks actresses are the lowest form of society."

A cannonball took up residence in Willow's chest. Poor Silas. She closed her eyes for a moment against the pain of prejudice. Why hadn't he told her any of this?

Alicia sniffed. "I don't feel that way, and I don't think the majority of the congregation would feel that way. It's just Mother has these odd ideas, and once she sets her mind on something, it's hard to get her to change it." She shook Willow's arm. "I think you're perfect for Silas. He's so nice, and he deserves to be happy. And he is so happy now that he's met you. He'll be a better minister, and the church will be better for his marrying you."

Willow savored the words for a moment, allowing them to soothe the hurt of Mrs. Drabble's dislike, but there was still the issue at hand to deal with. "Thank you. I hope what you say is true. Now that you've calmed down a bit, we should talk with Kenneth. He's worn a path in front of the cabin."

As they walked up the bank, Kenneth stopped pacing and shoved his hands into his pockets. "Are you going to go to her parents or the preacher?"

"No, but you should. Both of you." *Lord, help me be bold to speak the truth, but in a way that they will hear and respond to. Give me the words.* "Kenneth, it's plain to me you love Alicia dearly, and she clearly feels the same for you."

He nodded and put his arm around Alicia. "I'd do anything for her."

"If you truly love her, then you want to protect her from any harm. You're endangering her reputation and both of your characters by meeting like this." She swallowed and looked from one to the other. "If you continue, no good will come from it."

Kenneth rested his chin on Alicia's head. "How is it you know so much? You can't be any older than Alicia."

Willow sighed. "I'm right out of my depth here, but I'd hate to see you two ruin your lives. I've come to the conclusion that if God puts a fence around something, He means it to be there."

She glanced at the sun. "Alicia, it's getting late. We should go."

Kenneth's arm tightened around Alicia. His face twisted in anguish as he brushed a kiss across her temple and bent for a moment to rest his forehead on hers, as if afraid he might never be with her again.

As Alicia slipped from his arms, Willow offered one last plea. "Please, go see Silas again and explain everything. I'm sure he can help you both."

Walking along the stream bank, conscious of the need to hurry, Willow contemplated the young couple's situation. Had she helped the situation or only made it worse?

TEN

"And you're sure it's not a problem? Not with the board or with the church?" Willow smoothed her skirts, swaying to the rocking of the buggy. Worry over what his church thought had her tossing and turning most nights and fretting during the day until she couldn't wait any longer to broach the subject.

"Don't worry about it. Jesse and Matilda and Ned told me not to worry, and I'm telling you. Mrs. Drabble is a bit upset, but she'll get over it." Silas flicked the reins. "Jesse is proud of his mining operation. The minute I told him you'd never been in a silver mine, he insisted I bring you to his."

Willow let the matter rest, not wanting to mar their happiness with talk of unpleasant things. This afternoon was a gift, precious time with Silas, and she intended to make the most of it.

They pulled to a stop at the top of a steep

161

grade. Silas hopped from the buggy and came around to help her alight. "I'm glad Jesse provided the transportation, too. Since I live alone, I usually go everywhere I need to on foot or on horseback." He smiled. "Looks like I might need to see about getting another conveyance in the near future."

Willow bit her lower lip to control her smile. The warmth in his eyes spread through her clear to her toes. "I'm a little nervous. The thought of being so far underground with all that rock over my head . . ."

He squeezed her hand. "You don't have to go down if you don't want to."

"No, I do. And I wouldn't want to disappoint Mr. Mackenzie after he's been so generous. I'll be fine as long as you're with me."

Jesse stepped out onto the porch of a wooden building, spied them, and jumped down without bothering to use the steps. "You made it. Great. We just finished the shift change, so the bucket's free."

They followed him to an open-sided shed. Willow whispered to Silas. "The bucket?"

He winked. "They lower us into the mine via a big bucket. That's how they get the ore up, too. Then they load it into carts, and it travels on these tracks over to the stamp-mill." He pointed to the rails and ties leading away toward a tall building built into the side of the mountain from which pounding, grinding, crushing sounds rumbled and rolled. "They crush the rock there and use chemicals to extract the silver and lead and whatever other metals or minerals they are looking for."

Jesse motioned to a worker who pulled a lever, starting a clanking donkey engine and bringing an enormous metal container to the surface. "Here you go." He held out a hand to help Willow over the side.

Her heart lodged in her throat, and her mouth went paper dry. She tried not to think of all the empty space beneath her feet nor the darkness. What had come over her to say yes to this venture?

Silas swung his long legs over the rim of the bucket, setting it to swaying and making her stomach lurch. Jesse joined them, bringing a lantern along, and they began their descent. Yellow light bounced off jagged rock, and the chain rattled as it unwrapped from the winch overhead. Several pipes ran down the shaft.

Jesse pointed. "For pumping in clean air and pumping out water. Always a problem trying to keep a mine dry. There's talk of building a communal tunnel through the mountain someday to drain the mines above it."

Down, down, down. The farther they descended, the higher her heart rose in her throat.

Silas found her hand and slipped his arm around her waist. "You're freezing. Are you all right?"

She nodded. "It's rather . . . thrilling, isn't it?"

Jesse raised the lantern. "We'll go down about six hundred feet today. This shaft goes deeper, but we'll stop there and head into a side stope. My son, David, is the mine engineer, and he's got a nose for silver that puts every other engineer in the Rockies to shame. This stope is the richest we've ever brought in."

The bucket lurched to a stop beside a tunnel on Willow's right.

Jesse clambered out, holding the lantern high and reaching to help her. "Here we go. Watch your head, Silas."

Rock gritted under her shoes, and the whole place smelled like damp earth and dust. A trickle of water ran down the wall toward the vertical shaft and disappeared over the edge. At periodic intervals in the tunnel they walked, iron rings had been driven into the side walls at about head-high and held tallow candles that dripped onto the rocks below. The clink of metal on metal came to them, the sound magnified by ricocheting off the walls.

"Here we are." Jesse stopped beside two miners with pickaxes and metal hats. "We've cleared this tunnel after the last blast, and these men are drilling new holes for more explosives."

The miners straightened, their faces gleaming with sweat and streaked with dirt. They removed their gloves, and the taller one took a kerchief from his pocket and swiped his face. "Boss." He nodded. "It's pretty slow going through here, but we're making progress. Should be ready to blast tomorrow if everything goes well."

"Sounds good." Jesse blew out one of the candles, removed it from the holder, and hung the lantern in its place. "Boys, you know Pastor Hamilton? And this is Miss Starr. You might've heard of her, too. She's one of the actresses putting on the play at the new theater."

"Preacher." They nodded, but they didn't look at Silas. Their eyes were on her. Dirty, hardworking, smelling of earth and sweat and smoke. Hard rock miners. "Miss, it's a pleasure to meet you." The spokesman of the pair removed his hat to reveal a balding head, and the one who had yet to speak nearly tripped over his feet to shake her hand.

Francine would have a fit if she knew Willow was socializing with common laborers, but Willow didn't care. These men were the salt of the earth, as good as anybody and better than many of the people Francine sought approval from. She took his grimy hand, smiling. "I'm pleased to meet you. You've very brave working so far underground like this. Please, tell me what it is you're doing here. I've never been in a mine before, and I'm eager to learn."

Silas hid his smile, but he couldn't quell the satisfaction and pride he had in Willow. Her kind reception of a class of men she'd most likely not come into contact with before pleased him greatly. There she stood between two rough miners, listening avidly, accepting them for who they were and not worrying if she got her dress dirty.

The miners responded to her friendliness, telling her everything they could about what it was like to dig for precious metals in the bowels of the earth.

"The engineer tells us how deep to make the holes and in what pattern. When we've got it just right, the powder man sets the charges." The taller miner pointed and made twisting motions with his hands as if connecting fuses. "Then we clear the mine, and" — he made a plunging motion with his hands — "kaboom!"

The shorter miner, not to be outdone, elbowed closer. "After the dust settles, we come back in and start clearing the rock. Out it goes to the shaft and up to the stamp mill, and there you go. In the end, they have lovely silver pigs."

"Pigs?"

He rubbed his nose with the back of his hand. "Yep, when they're done extracting the metal at the stamp mill, they pour it into bars called pigs. Then they ship them out by rail to places where they refine it and turn it into teaspoons and sugar tongs and the like."

Jesse tugged on Silas's sleeve and pulled him aside. "She's great with them. I wondered how she'd take to the workers, but you'd think she'd been with them all her life."

"She's interested in people. Just like she was with the Sunday school boys. Treats everyone the same."

"She'll make you a fine little wife if you can get Mrs. Drabble off your back. She hasn't let up about you courting an actress.

I've tried, and Matilda has tried to get her to see reason, even to go to the play and see for herself there's nothing objectionable in it, but she won't budge. She truly believes the theater is wicked and so is everyone associated with it."

Silas loosened his jaw muscles. "Thanks for trying. I'll confess I'm at a loss to know how to continue. I've tried to apologize and let her know I have no ill feelings toward her, but she is adamant that she is right, and nothing short of total capitulation on my part will satisfy her."

"That kind of narrow thinking tends to sow discord in a congregation. I've seen things like this cause such a rift between folks that a church fractures. I don't want that sort of thing to happen in this church. They're a fine group of folks, but having Mrs. Drabble dripping her unhappiness into everyone's ears is bound to have an effect."

"What do you think we should do about it? I can't give up Willow just to make Mrs. Drabble happy, but what if the church comes apart? What if the district supervisor is of the same mind as Mrs. Drabble and forces me to choose between Willow and the church?" The very thought had kept him awake for hours each night, praying, searching his heart and the scriptures.

Jesse leaned his shoulder against the wall and crossed his arms, the lantern light flickering across his face and making shadows. "I'd hate to have to make this a matter of church discipline, but the truth is she's gossiping and spreading ill feelings, and she's not respecting the authority of the pastor. If I thought for a moment she had a real issue, if you were doing something contrary to scripture or detrimental to the church, I'd be the first to come to you with it. But you're not doing anything wrong by courting Willow. She's a believer, right?"

"Yes. I made sure before I asked to call on her."

"And she's a good girl — anyone who has spent five minutes with her can see that. She's kind and generous and sweet. A woman a man could be proud to call his wife. Matilda likes her, and I'd back my wife's judgment anytime. Mrs. Drabble needs to stop what she's doing and leave you two alone, or there's going to be real trouble."

As they rode the bucket back to the surface, Silas tried to ignore the heavy, churning feeling in his gut. Real trouble in his church. How could he avoid it and keep Willow? He was sure she was the one God wanted him to marry, but how could he if it meant dividing his church? He'd been called to be a pastor. He couldn't fail his parishioners, not even Mrs. Drabble.

When they stood in the bright sunshine again, Willow breathed deeply, turning her face to the warm rays. "I'm so glad to be out of there. I could never work in a mine. I'd suffocate."

"I wouldn't have guessed, the way you were talking to those miners. Thank you for being so nice to them. They'll be talking about it for a long time."

Jesse blew out the lantern and returned it to a shelf in the shed. "Before I forget, I wanted to thank you for the tickets for the men."

"Tickets?" Silas's eyebrows rose.

"Yep, she's giving tickets to all the Mackenzie miners over the next week or so." Jesse grinned. "A block of ten front-row seats every night this week."

Silas reached for her hand. "That's very generous of you."

Her cheeks went a little pink, and she shrugged. "I wanted to show my appreciation to Jesse and to the workers for letting me tour the mine. Jesse, they can call for the tickets at the window. I'll let them know in the office."

"And I'll deliver the tickets to Mrs.

Drabble like you want, but don't get your hopes up."

Silas took Willow's hand. "What's this?"

She shrugged. "I thought if only she would come to the theater and see for herself what the play was like, and maybe come to the reception afterward, she could see we're not evil people bent on dragging God-fearing folks to destruction. It's worth a try, anyway."

ELEVEN

Willow took Silas's helping hand and climbed out of the buggy behind the rear stage door. She smiled at the guard posted there and stepped into the familiar area of the theater away from the stage, breathing in the scents of fabric, dust, makeup, and kerosene lamps. Everything known and familiar.

Silas closed the side door behind them and put his hand to the small of her back to guide her through the hallway. "We aren't late, are we?"

Willow edged around an open trunk frothing with costumes and props and stepped over a rolled-up canvas backdrop. "Someone needs to organize these things better. We're constantly tripping over equipment. And no, we're not late." Glancing through the open door of her dressing room, she spied Clement and Francine deep in conversation.

Not wanting to intrude, she tugged Silas's hand, drawing him toward the wings of stage left. The indigo velvet drapes surrounded them. "I used to watch my mother every night from the wings when I was a little girl. The feel of velvet always brings back those memories." In the low light of the preperformance theater, she studied his face.

"I wish I had known you as a little girl. You must've been adorable, all big eyes and ringlets. Did you always want to act? Did you dream of taking the stage?" He took her hands and drew her toward him.

"No, not really, but it was all I knew. For Francine it is a burning passion, and one she and my mother shared. I think Mother never really knew what to do with me. Francine says I was a homely child, awkward and clumsy. Francine was ten when I was born, and I guess I was a bit of a surprise to my parents. They thought they were done having children. Then my father passed away, and my mother had two girls to support with her acting. When she died, it was just Francine and me. Francine lives for the stage and the fame and the starring roles. And I . . ." She swallowed. "I feel like I have just been existing, putting in time, until now."

He brushed the hair away from her temple, his touch as soft as mist. "So you might be happy away from the stage? You could be content in another way of life?"

"It would depend on what that other way of life was, but yes, I could be very happy away from the stage." Willow breathed deeply, inhaling his scent — soap and sunshine and Silas.

"Hmmm." His voice rumbled deep in his throat, and he eased his arms around her waist. "What if that life was with me?"

Her hands went up his lapels and twined around his neck. "Then I think I could be very happy indeed."

He bent his head, brushing her lips with his, sending a shock through her. Her eyelids fluttered closed, and his embrace tightened. Again his lips caressed hers, and then more forcefully as if he wanted to consume her. She poured all the love in her heart into that kiss where it met his love like the crashing of a wave on a rocky shore.

Never had she expected to find something like this, so powerful, so precious, so perfect.

When the kiss ended, he continued to hold her close, his breath harsh against her cheek.

"Willow Starr, I love you as I've never loved anyone. Please say you'll marry me.

Say you love me and you'll share my life forever."

Her hands came up to cup his cheeks, and she looked deeply into his dark brown eyes, as velvety as his voice. She swallowed, trying to absorb all the wonderful sensations coursing through her, wanting to remember everything. The feeling that together they could conquer anything, that they could tackle any problem and come out the victors, swept over her. Worries about his church and her acting company slipped away, drowned by the love in his eyes and her heart. "Yes, Silas, yes. I love you, and I will marry you." She could've stayed there in his arms all evening, but a clatter of footsteps and the sound of voices forced them apart.

Silas, as if reluctant to break contact with her, raised her fingers to his lips, planting a kiss across her knuckles before turning her hand over to place a kiss in her palm. He closed her fingers and squeezed, winking at her. "I'll be watching the performance tonight. You'd best get changed and ready before someone comes looking." He turned her around to head her in the right direction. "I'm going to nip home and change, but I'll be back."

Her mind still spinning and her heart full

to bursting, she nodded and made her way to her dressing room. Clement and Francine had vanished, which was just as well. She couldn't have borne it if her sister made some condescending or trite comment that rubbed the bloom off the moment.

She stepped into her costume for the first act and fumbled with the buttons, her hands shaking. An uncontrollable urge to dance, to laugh, to sing, to somehow let the entire world know of her happiness kept breaking over her. And when she sat at her dressing table to arrange her hair and put on her makeup, the stars in her eyes dazzled her. She wore the unmistakable look of love.

Silas couldn't stop grinning. He hurried to the parsonage, grateful to still have the loan of Jesse's horse and buggy, though the time he saved in travel was eaten up by having to unhitch and turn the horse out into the glebe. A hasty wash, fresh shirt, and carefully knotted tie, and he was on his way back to the theater on foot.

Following Willow's instructions, he bypassed the still-locked front doors and entered at the side of the building under the knowing eyes of a stagehand. "Evening, parson. You're back quick. Gonna be a good show tonight."

Silas nodded. "Thanks, Bill."

The hallway bustled with cast members and crew as curtain time approached. He navigated the props and scenery stacked along the hallway, flicking a glance at Willow's closed dressing-room door as he edged past a man in a frock coat. He recognized the actor as St. John in the play. At least it wasn't that rather oily fellow who played Rochester. Something about him raised Silas's hackles. He chuckled. Unreasonable, really. Projecting his jealousy of Willow onto the circumstances of the play. He paused to allow two stagehands carrying a desk between them to pass.

"Excuse me, are you Willow's friend? The preacher?"

Silas swiveled to locate the voice. A slender, pale man in a tan checked suit leaned back in a chair in a side room.

"Yes. I'm Pastor Hamilton."

"Come in. I was hoping I'd get a chance to speak with you soon." The man rose and held out his hand. "Clement Nielson. Director."

Silas shook his hand. "Willow speaks very highly of you."

"I'm glad. I think quite a bit of her myself, which is what I wanted to talk to you about." He motioned to an empty chair and resumed his own. "Has she told you about the offers she's received to play Juliet this fall in New York? A starring role in one of the biggest theaters in the country. It's the opportunity of a lifetime."

Silas sat up and leaned forward a bit. "This fall? New York . . . as in city?"

"That's right. You can't imagine the prestige that comes along with a role like this, especially if the actress can deliver the goods. And Willow can. She's the most gifted, natural actress it has been my privilege to work with, and she will be the darling of the New York theater crowd. Money, fame, the best of everything. It's all waiting for her."

Silas struggled to grasp the significance of the director's words. New York, this fall? But what did that mean for him? Willow had only an hour before agreed to be his wife. "Has she accepted?"

"No, and that's what I want to talk to you about. I've put it to Willow, and she's been silent on the subject ever since. An added pressure is that without Willow's consent, none of us are going to New York. I told her to take her time and really consider the options, but our time's running out. I have to know her answer, and I'm afraid of what it will be."

Silas gripped his knees, his mind reeling. "She hasn't mentioned any of this to me."

"You'll be wondering what my stake is in all this." Clement picked up a letter opener from the desk and toyed with it. "When I first told Willow of the offer, I suggested she needed a manager, and I proposed myself for the job. She would need someone who truly had her best interests at heart to look out for her in the big city." He quirked his eyebrow. "As you can imagine, Francine is far from being that person. I proposed myself for a couple of reasons. First, I truly do care about Willow. She's a wonderful young woman who hasn't had the easiest job being Francine's sister. And second, Willow's father was my best friend, and I promised him I would look out after his girls."

A stagehand knocked on the half-open door. "Five minutes to curtain."

"Thank you, Mel. Now" — Clement continued as if he hadn't been interrupted — "you're probably thinking that I would push Willow to accept the role, go to New York, and make us all famous, but you'd be wrong. I've watched Willow the past few weeks since she met you, and I can say without reservation, I've never seen her happier. It's like she's all lit up inside. I think she wants a home and a family more than she wants anything, and I think you're just the man to provide her with those things. She's not cut out for the big city and all the demands she would meet there. I want her to be happy, and I think she's happy with you."

Silas sat back, stunned by this turn of events. "That's very big of you."

The director shrugged and pushed himself up. "I just wanted to warn you. Francine won't take this lightly. I'll do what I can to protect Willow, and you need to do the same. It might be best if you eloped before Francine could do anything about it."

Though the idea strongly appealed to Silas, he shook his head. "No, I won't marry Willow on the sly, as if we were doing something wrong. I have a ministry and a congregation to consider. We'll be married in the church and in the presence of our friends. She agreed just today to be my wife."

"I guess that means I'll have to tell New York and this acting company that Willow is retiring from the stage." Clement shoved his hands into his pockets. "On the one hand, it's too bad. The theater is losing a great actress, but on the other, I'm very happy for you. Congratulations. But watch out for Francine. She's not a woman who enjoys being thwarted, and she was counting on New York."

Silas made his way to the balcony box seat Willow had reserved for him, his mind in turmoil. He was grateful and flattered that Willow had chosen him over such a fantastic opportunity, because it meant she must truly love him, and he was glad he hadn't known about the offer before he'd proposed.

The sweet memory of her kiss, of her arms around his neck and her fingers tangling in his hair, of holding her close swept over him. And just as sweet, her declaration of love and promise to be his wife. He needed to make plans to tell his congregation soon.

Which meant informing Mrs. Drabble. He scanned the boxes and seats, hoping Mrs. Drabble had accepted Willow's peace offering and attended the play, but he couldn't see her anywhere. A knot squirmed in his stomach.

The curtain went up, and the play began. True to her word, Willow had reserved seats on the front row, and a group of miners and their wives sat together, faces rapt. She was so generous and sweet, surely once the congregation took the time to get to know her all reservations would be dropped and they would embrace her and accept her as

181

his bride.

Once more her performance took his breath away, and she played the part of a young woman in love so well he had to quell his jealousy of Mr. Rochester again. At the conclusion, the audience surged to its feet. The miners were especially enthusiastic, stomping and whistling, bringing the cast back again and again for curtain calls, though it was Willow's name they shouted the loudest.

Her eyes met his. A flush decorated her cheeks, and her eyes shone. She waved to him, and with refreshing spontaneity, she blew him a kiss, which set the audience into another uproar. He couldn't wait to be with her again. They had so much to talk about, and if he could manage it, he planned to get at least one more kiss before saying good night.

He made his way down the stairs. When he reached the foyer, he was surrounded by the men he'd met at the Mackenzie mine earlier that day. They pumped his hand, grinning, introducing their wives and girl-friends, thanking him and asking him to be sure to pass their thanks along to Willow for the tickets. Best time they'd ever had, and wasn't she something?

Silas wholeheartedly agreed. It was all he

could do not to announce to every person he saw that Willow was his fiancée. A steam engine of anticipation surged away in his chest. He couldn't wait to see her again. Though he wanted to bolt around to the back of the building and wait for her at the stage door, he couldn't be rude to these men. Anyway, it would take her some time to change. Telling himself to be patient didn't make the wait any easier.

One of the miners shoved his hands into his back pockets and lowered his voice to speak just to Silas. "Reverend, I haven't made much of a point of going to church in the past few years, but after meeting you and Miss Starr, you can count on me being in the front row come Sunday morning. And I know a lot of the other fellows feel the same. Most high-quality folks like Miss Starr wouldn't bother to spit on hard-rock miners if they was on fire, but she was kindness itself. If she wasn't so sweet on you, and I wasn't old enough to be her pappy, I'd go after her myself. You're a lucky man." He grinned, deepening the lines on his face.

"Blessed. I'm a blessed man." Silas nodded. Here was proof positive for the congregation that Willow would be an asset to his ministry. Come Sunday morning, everyone

would see what a perfect pastor's wife she
would make.

Twelve

The applause, especially from her guests in the front row, thundered through the performance hall and made the lamplight flicker. It was hard not to respond to such wholehearted approval. Her cheeks hurt from smiling. Philip held her hand on one side and Francine on the other as they bowed, answering yet another curtain call. With each trip back onto the stage, her sister's grip tightened until Willow's fingers stung. She finally extricated herself from them both to wave and accept the flowers the miners offered from the edge of the stage. Her eyes sought Silas's in the balcony, and the warm pride and love in his expression echoed louder in her heart than the applause of the crowd.

The minute she stepped out of view of the audience after the last round of cheering, she blew out a big sigh. How she'd managed to remember her lines and hit her marks, she didn't know, since all she could think about all evening was Silas and his proposal. And his kiss.

She was getting married. Squealing and hopping around probably wasn't the best way to express her happiness, but she was very tempted. A giggle erupted as she tried to imagine what Francine would say at such a display. Willow decided to save the squealing and hopping until she could be alone.

Cast and crew thronged the wings, their conversations washing around her like a tide. She caught sight of Francine disappearing into Clement's office. Good, she'd have the dressing room all to herself.

Though her blood sang in her veins and she had a feeling she could fly right up to the catwalk with happiness, the draining of strength that always followed a performance had begun. A quick glance at the clock as she entered the room told her she should hurry, or Silas would be kept waiting. She laid aside the flowers and stepped behind the screen in the corner to rid herself of her costume.

Once into her own clothes, it was a matter of minutes to remove hairpins, brush out the severe style, and pin it up in her natural, loose knot. Clasping her string of pearls around her neck, she ran her fingers over the cool beads. A little ache pinched her heart. She wished her father were here. He would've loved Silas.

Glancing at the clock, she reached for her handbag. He must be at the stage door by now.

A knock sounded. Silas. Grinning, she ran to open it. "I'm sorry to keep you wait—" She stopped, deflated.

Philip.

"What do you want?"

"What kind of greeting is that?"

"Francine isn't here. I think she's in Clement's office."

"I didn't come to see Francine."

"Well, I hope you didn't come to see me, because I've got to go. I'm meeting someone." She held on to the edge of the door, waiting for him to step back.

"That goody-goody preacher? I don't understand what you see in him, and I never would've expected a pastor to enjoy a little springtime dalliance. I bet you thought no one saw you throwing yourself at him in the wings before tonight's performance. I have to say, you surprised me with your . . . ardor?"

Her cheeks flamed, and her throat tightened. He'd seen? Who else? Her hand went to her throat and tangled in her necklace.

A sneer smeared Philip's mouth. "Still, you live and learn. I hope you don't break his heart when this play is done and we move on to New York."

"For your information, when *Jane Eyre* finishes its run, I'm not going to New York. I'll be staying with that 'goody-goody preacher' who has asked me to marry him. And his name is Silas Hamilton. You may call him Reverend Hamilton."

Fire shot into Philip's eyes, and he put his hand flat on the door, pushing his way inside the dressing room and forcing her back. He closed the door behind him. "What are you talking about? You can't possibly mean to stay in this backwater with that no-account pulpit pounder. What about New York? What about me?"

Anger sizzled in her veins at his maligning of Silas. "You don't enter into this at all. And Silas isn't a no-account. He's worth a dozen of you with change left over, you arrogant toad. Now get out of here. You shouldn't be in a lady's dressing room." She pointed to the door.

His scowl deepened, and she moistened her dry lips. Fury emanated from him in waves, and she backed up another step.

"Arrogant toad?" In two strides he crossed the small open space and grabbed her wrist.

"So, you'll share your favors with the preacher, but not with me? Well, if you won't share, I'll just take what I want."

"Let me go, Philip. You're going to re-gre—"

She understood his intent a fraction of a second before his lips came down on hers. His hand clamped on her jaw, and he pushed her up against the wall. Pummeling his shoulder with her free fist, she struggled to break the kiss, but he paid no heed to the blows, and she was pinned so effectively she couldn't get a good swing. His lips squished against hers, and his hands maintained their iron grip. His solid body blocked any escape attempt, pressing against her.

Why didn't someone come? Where was Francine?

Silas. Where are you, Silas?

Tears stung her eyes. Keeping her lips rigid, she let herself go limp, hoping to catch Philip off guard. He raised his head and stroked the hair at her temple. "That's it, my sweet. I knew you'd give in to me if you just gave yourself the chance."

Gathering all her strength, she shoved against his chest, forcing him backward using the wall for leverage. "I'll never give in to you. If you ever lay a hand on me again, I'll scream." She bolted for the door, but

189

her feet tangled in her hem, slowing her down.

Philip grabbed her around the waist and flung her down on the chaise Francine used for preperformance naps. She bounced and scrambled, trying to evade his clutching hands. When his face loomed over hers, she slapped it as hard as she could.

"Why, you little —" He caught her wrist, and she let out a shriek.

The door flew open and hit the wall like a rifle shot. "Willow?"

"Silas!"

In an instant, concern, comprehension, and anger crossed his face. He was on Philip in a single leap, tearing the actor away from Willow.

Philip swung his fist, connected with Silas's left eye, and sent him reeling. Turning back to Willow, who had frozen at the sight of her beloved storming to her rescue, Philip reached for her again. "I'll show you, you little minx."

She scrambled off the chaise, clutching for something, anything to ward him off. Her fingers closed around the vase standing ready for flowers.

Before she could swing it around, Silas's arms came around Philip's shoulders, dragging him away from her. Staggering, they crashed into the wall. The impact loosened Silas's grip, and Philip swung around on him.

Silas was ready. His fist smacked into Philip's jaw, dropping him into a heap on the floor. His chest heaved, and his eyes sought Willow's.

People crowded into the doorway, headed by Francine. "What on earth is going on here?" Her imperious voice cut the air.

Willow let the vase slip from her hands, and it met disaster, shattering near Philip's head and bathing him in china bits and cold water.

He groaned, roused by the dousing.

Willow ignored him and flew to Silas.

His arms opened, and he gathered her close. "Are you all right? He didn't hurt you?" He whispered the words against her hair, and she raised her hands to cover her face, shaking and shivering in spite of his embrace. His heart thundered under her ear, and his breathing rasped.

"Willow, please, tell me if you're hurt." He raised her face and peeled her hands away.

Looking into his eyes, she bit her lip and shook her head. Featherlight, she touched his eyebrow and the swelling already starting there. "I'm not hurt. But your eye." By tomorrow he'd have a purple shiner.

Movement behind her made her turn her head. She placed her palms on Silas's chest to steady herself. Philip groaned again and lurched to his feet, assisted by one of the stagehands.

Clement elbowed into the room. "What is all this?" He looked from Silas to Philip and back. "Moncrieff, what have you done?"

"Why are you blaming Philip?" Francine asked, her cheeks red and eyes snapping. "He's the injured party here. That man knocked him right out."

Clement put his hands on his hips, very much the boss and commander. "Well?"

Philip put on a martyred air and touched his jaw, wincing. "It was just a little misunderstanding."

Silas gathered himself to protest, and Willow tugged on his lapels. "Don't," she whispered. "Just get me out of here, please?"

His arms tightened, and his eyebrows came down — well, one came down, the other was too swollen. "You're sure?"

She nodded and moved to his side. He kept his arm around her waist.

Clement studied them for a moment and turned to the faces in the doorway. "All right, get moving, folks. The excitement's over."

Reluctantly, the doorway emptied. Philip cast Willow a black look and made for the hall.

Clement stopped him. "I'd like a word with you in my office, Moncrieff. I'll be there shortly."

Philip's footsteps could be heard all the way down the hall, and a door slammed.

Willow relaxed, sagging into Silas's side.

"Willow, what is the meaning of this? Two men brawling in our dressing room? Look at this mess." Francine waved toward the broken glass, the water puddle, and the costume rack now toppled onto the floor. "And what did you do to my chaise?" The lounge had been knocked askew and all the pillows scattered in the melee.

"Francine, perhaps now isn't the best time." Clement put his hand under her elbow. "I'll send someone to clean this up. For now, perhaps you'd like a cup of tea? I know these little upsets can be stressful for such a high-strung, creative talent as yours."

At his placating, solicitous tone, Francine lost a bit of her imperiousness. "Yes, I could use a cup of tea." She took his arm and allowed herself to be led away.

At the last minute she looked back over her shoulder. "Willow, we will discuss this later." And her expression boded ill for Willow's already fragile peace of mind.

Silas let Willow push him into a chair, though he should have been the one comforting her.

She went to the pitcher on the stand in the corner, wet a cloth, and brought it back. "Your poor eye. Does it hurt?"

"No, I'm fine." He took the cloth and held it against the sting. "I'm more concerned about you. What happened?"

She blew out a breath and crossed her arms at her waist.

A shudder shook her, and he reached for her hand, drawing her down until he held her on his lap like a little girl. Smoothing her disheveled hair away from her face, he asked again, "What happened? You can tell me."

"We were . . . arguing, I guess. He saw us before the play — when you proposed." A delicate flush pinked her cheeks, and she swallowed. "I guess it made him angry. He's made advances before, and I've always put him off."

His arm tightened around her waist. Advances? He wanted to punch the scoundrel again. Though not a man of violence — Silas couldn't remember ever punching anyone before — the strength of his protective fury surprised him. He didn't regret knocking Philip Moncrieff out one bit.

She tucked her head onto his shoulder. "I told him I was going to marry you, and I called him —" She broke off, embarrassment coloring her words. "I called him," she whispered, her breath brushing against his neck, "an arrogant toad."

He wanted to laugh. His gentle, sweet Willow a spitfire? Keeping his voice even so she wouldn't think he was laughing at her, he said, "And that made him mad."

"Very. He said if I wouldn't share my kisses with him, he'd just take what he wanted." She sat up, her gray eyes inches from his. "I really think he only wanted a kiss, but I fought him, and he seemed to lose control. Things got out of hand so fast. I'm glad you came through that door when you did."

"I am, too." Silas wanted to drop a kiss on her adorable nose, but he forced himself to refrain. "What happens now? Will Philip be fired?"

She studied her hands in her lap. "I don't know. It will depend on what Philip tells Clement. There isn't anyone in the cast who can take over Philip's role as Mr. Rochester. Though I wish there was someone. I can't stand pretending to be in love with him in the play. It was bad before. It will be nauseating now."

"You can't think to continue after what happened tonight?"

"I have to. I have a contract with the company, and no matter what happens behind the scenes, I have to honor it. The show is the most important thing, and over the next three weeks, I *am* Jane Eyre. I won't let Philip prevent me from doing my job."

Determination stared out of her eyes, and while he admired her grit, the thought of her enduring the presence of that cad for twenty-one more days twisted his innards. He planned then and there to have a talk with both Clement and Bill, the guard at the back door, about seeing that nobody, especially Philip, bothered Willow again. And as much as he was able, he'd be at every performance to see she got to the hotel safely. "What about Francine? What will you tell her?"

"I'll tell her the truth about what happened, but I don't expect her to take it well."

"Have you told her about our engagement?" Just saying it aloud pleased him. Made it more official. She took the wet cloth from his hand and dabbed at his eye.

Her fussing pleased him, too. It was nice to have someone care about him.

She caught sight of the back of his hand and gave a little squeak. "Oh, your knuckles."

He glanced at the split skin, bruised knuckles, and swelling. Philip's jaw had felt like punching an anvil. He flexed his fingers, trying not to wince.

She dabbed at the cut, her lower lip tucked behind her front teeth. The soft crooning sounds she made sounded sympathetic and contrite at the same time.

He caught her hand to still her ministrations. "My hand will be fine. Did you tell Francine about our engagement?"

"I haven't told her yet. There wasn't time before the show, and you'll think I'm silly, but I wanted to . . . I don't know, savor it for a while before I let anyone else know." She folded and refolded the damp cloth.

"I don't think that's silly at all, though I admit I had just the opposite reaction. I wanted to shout it from the housetops. I wanted to yell it from the balcony the minute the play ended." Eyeing the open door, he stole a quick kiss. "Clement told me about the job offer from New York. Honey, I want you to be sure, really sure you would rather marry me than accept that role." Though it raked his heart to say it, he knew he had to. "I don't want you to have any regrets."

Her eyes widened. "He told you?"

"It's a big decision, affecting not just your future but the entire company. You know I want you to stay here and marry me, but I can't ask that of you unless you're very sure. Especially since not everyone will be happy if you turn it down."

She twined her arms around his neck and rested her head on his shoulder. "Silas, I'm sure. I've never been so sure. New York has nothing I need. Everything I want is right here." She pressed her hand to his chest just over his heart.

His throat lurched, and he tightened his hold. "I'd better get you to the hotel before it gets too late. Considering everything that's happened, I think the sooner we announce our engagement the better. Sunday morning — two days from now — after the morning service, I'll let the church know." Ignoring the thrust of worry at what some of the church members might say, he hugged her. "Let's get you home."

The desire to protect her nearly overwhelmed him, and it was getting harder and harder to drop her off at the hotel each night. They needed to decide on a wedding date, and whenever it would be looked a long way off to him.

THIRTEEN

"I won't have it. You're going to get this nonsense out of your head and accept that offer, and that's that." Francine sat propped up against the head of the bed, her hair in twin plaits on her shoulders and her face a mask of white cream. She rubbed goose grease into her hands from a small pot on her lap. "And causing a row with Philip? Whatever did you say to lead him on that way?"

Willow put the brush on the dressing table and met her sister's eyes in the mirror. "I did nothing to lead him on. Philip didn't need any encouragement from me. He's been pestering me for some time, and he finally got what he deserved."

"You must've done something. Philip wouldn't have given you so much as a nod otherwise. It's just like you to try to steal him from me."

"Steal him?" Willow turned on the bench.

"I didn't realize he belonged to you. I don't want him. You can have him gift-wrapped for all I care, though you'd be foolish. He's a cad and a rogue, and I can't wait to be away from him."

"You're not fooling me. Playing one man against another. Did you feel triumphant when they fought over you?"

"I was appalled and grateful to Silas for coming to my aid. Philip deserved to be trounced, and he was. If you'd heard what he said to me, what he tried to do to me, you wouldn't be so eager to defend him."

"You're being melodramatic, as usual. I'm sure the situation could've been resolved with a few words instead of fists. Philip will be furious. And he has every right to be. I'm so angry with you I could scream. You're just being selfish not taking the job in New York. How can you be so stupid?"

"It's not stupid to fall in love. I love Silas, he loves me, and we're getting married."

"But what about me? What about the company?"

"The company got along just fine before I came along, and it will do just fine without me. New York isn't the only place Clement got offers from, and he'll book you somewhere for the fall. I thought you'd be happy I was leaving. You've done nothing but gripe about me getting the lead in *Jane Eyre.* With me staying here, you'll have top billing again."

"Don't do me any favors." Francine tugged gloves over her greasy hands and slammed the pot of goose grease onto the bedside table. The crystals hanging from the lamp swayed as she swung her feet out of bed. "Clement will sign us up for some other mining town or cow camp, and I'll never get to New York."

"There's no saying you have to stay with this company. You could try New York on your own."

"A lot you know. If you'd take this offer, we'd all arrive there with jobs and lodgings and a bit of security. I can't just pack a bag and head off not knowing what might happen. This company is all I have, all I've known, and I can't leave it on the off chance I might find work somewhere else." Desperation colored Francine's voice, and guilt pinched Willow's chest. "You're ruining my dreams." A sob caught in her throat.

Willow sent up a quick prayer for help but backed it up with a prayer for strength of purpose. "Francine, I'm sorry. I really am, but I have to follow my dreams. I can't go against what I know is right for me, what I feel God calling me to do."

Francine jerked and clutched the bed-clothes on either side of her. "Don't play that God card. You're doing this because it's what you want, not because of any God thing. You'd stay here just to spite me, whether Silas was a preacher or a street sweeper. But this isn't over. The whole company will know by now you've turned down the role and denied them their chance to make it big."

The thought of facing everyone tomorrow, knowing they'd be disappointed, made Willow quail, but she stiffened her resolve. She was doing the right thing. It wasn't fair of the producers in New York to put such responsibility on her, and Clement should've come to her with the offer in private before he told everyone else. Though at the time, she supposed he never would've thought she'd say no. Still, she had to do what she thought was right.

Francine glared, sliding back under the covers, jerking the quilt around. She didn't wait for Willow to get into bed before she turned out the light. "You're going to be sorry."

Willow barely caught her sister's mutter, and a shiver went up her spine.

Silas, too keyed up to sleep after leaving

Willow at the hotel, went to the church instead of the parsonage. He could always find something that needed doing there. His eye stung, and the lid was so swollen it obscured his vision, but he didn't have a shred of regret he'd defended Willow's honor with his fists.

Lighting the wall sconces, he circled the perimeter of the room, delighting in the comfortable, familiar feel of the room. A peace he could only find here invaded his soul.

Lord, thank You for bringing me to this place, for all the hurdles and mountains I had to climb over to get here. Thank You for the people of this church who challenge and enrich and encourage me. Help me to be the pastor You want me to be and the pastor they need me to be to help them grow and glorify You.

The oft-repeated prayer ran through his head. The burden of being the spiritual leader to this diverse group of believers weighed on him, but it was a pleasant weight most of the time. He knew he wasn't up to the task alone, but with God's help, he would do the best he could. And not only God's help, but soon Willow's, too. No more coming home to an empty house, no more being unable to offer hospitality, no more discussing church issues with the cat.

He grabbed a dustcloth and began on the left side of the church wiping down the pews. His congregants were creatures of habit, and each family usually sat in the same place week after week. As he progressed down the row, he prayed for the members as he came to their customary seats.

When he got to the Drabble pew, right side, second row, he knelt and put his elbows on the seat. This prayer was going to take more time than could be accomplished in a quick wipe-down.

"Lord, thank You for bringing the Drabbles to this church. Thank You for the acts of service they perform that edify the church and help us share Your Gospel with this community." He swallowed. Easy part done.

"Father, I ask You to help me to heal the rift between Mrs. Drabble and myself. These hard feelings have broken our fellowship and are detrimental to the church and Your name. Help me to forgive her, and humble me to ask her forgiveness. We need Your healing here to kill our pride and help us to submit and serve one another in love."

The front door scraped on the floor, reminding him he needed to remove it from the hinges and plane the bottom. Breaking off his prayer with a hasty "Amen," Silas lifted his head to look over the back of the pew.

"Pastor Hamilton? Are you in here?" Kenneth Hayes.

"Over here." He stood, dusting his knees.

Kenneth let out a breath. "Oh, good. I sorta panicked when the parsonage was dark. What happened to your eye?"

Touching the swelling, Silas winced at the pain. "It's nothing. A little difference of opinion."

Kenneth stared as if fascinated. "What's the other guy look like?"

Worse than me, I imagine. "What can I do for you? I've missed you in church the past couple of weeks." The less said about his altercation at the theater, the better. All sorts of rumors might start flying around, and he didn't want things to get blown out of proportion.

Dusky red crept around Kenneth's collar, and he ducked his head. "Well, I'm sorry, but I came here to do something about that." He returned to the front door and held out his hand. "He's here. C'mon in."

He drew a woman into the room, and Silas's eyes went wide. Alicia Drabble. A few puzzle pieces clicked together in his brain. Kenneth's certainty his ladylove's parents wouldn't relent, and Alicia's going toe to toe with her mother over dinner and being set down. Alicia kept her eyes lowered.

"It's awfully late for you two to be out together, isn't it?" Silas stepped into the aisle. Mrs. Drabble would have a conniption. "Alicia, your folks will be worried."

Kenneth squared his shoulders. "They don't need to worry about her any longer. Alicia and I are eloping, and we want you to perform the ceremony."

"Eloping?" Silas dropped his dustcloth.

Kenneth wrapped his arm around Alicia and hugged her to his side. "Don't try to stop us. If you won't do the honors, we'll ride over to the next town, and the next, and the next, until we find a preacher to marry us."

"Let's sit down and at least talk about this."

"No, our minds are made up. It has to be tonight." Kenneth's jaw set, and his eyes narrowed a bit.

"Alicia?"

"Please, Silas." She still didn't look at him. "I'm not going back to my parents' house without a wedding ring and marriage certificate. I can't." Desperation smothered her voice, and she turned her face into Kenneth's shoulder.

"It's really important we get married tonight. We *need* to get married." Kenneth's expression begged Silas to understand.

Alicia choked on a sob.

Silas's mind circled the implications and ramifications as he motioned for them to sit in one of the pews. His heart sat like a cold rock in his chest. Marriage should be a joyous time of celebration with friends and family, not a covert, desperate matter conducted in the middle of the night.

When they were seated he took the pew in front of them, turning sideways and laying his arm across the back. "Now, explain to me so there are no misunderstandings just why you have to get married tonight without the blessing of Alicia's parents."

They both stared at the floor. Kenneth reached over and clasped Alicia's clenched hands in her lap. "I did like you said and went to her folks again, but they refused to let me see Alicia. So we arranged to sneak out so we could be together."

"I see."

Alicia raised her chin. Her eyes swam with tears. "But you knew, didn't you? Didn't Willow tell you? She saw us together not long ago. I was sure she'd tell you all about it."

"She didn't say a word." Silas rubbed his jaw.

"Don't be mad at her. She said she wouldn't lie to you, and that you would have to know, but she wanted us to be the ones to tell you. I'm sure she wasn't going to keep it from you forever. Willow told us we'd get in trouble if we didn't stop meeting like that." Alicia blinked, sending the tears down her cheeks. "And she was right. We should've listened. She told us to come to you for help. And yesterday . . ."

Kenneth took a deep breath and looked Silas right in the eye. "Yesterday our feelings got the better of us. We stumbled. It was my fault. Please don't blame Alicia. We're both sorry, and we're here to make it right. We need to get married as soon as possible."

Silas grimaced and sent up a prayer for wisdom. "That certainly puts a new light on things. Would you be willing to wait until morning, and we could all three go to Alicia's parents and talk this out?"

"No. They'll contrive some way to keep us from getting married. They'll send Alicia away." Kenneth leaned forward, gripping the pew in front of him. "If you won't do it, we'll find someone else. She's not going back. We're both adults. We can make up our own minds. We'd like to have her parents' blessing, but we don't need their permission."

Silas rubbed his forehead, forgetting his black eye until he touched it. Mrs. Drabble was going to explode. And yet, what Kenneth said was true. They were old enough to choose for themselves, and they had excellent and expedient reasons for marrying in haste. "If you're sure about this, I would rather perform the ceremony myself than send you to someone else. But I have a few things to say first."

Kenneth nodded. "We figured you would."

"You both understand you've chosen a hard road. By giving in to temptation, you're starting out your marriage under a cloud. And" — Silas swallowed and took a deep breath — "there could be other consequences."

"We've talked about that. That's one of the reasons we want to get married as soon as possible."

"There's also the matter of Alicia's parents. You are both old enough to marry without their permission, but Alicia is their daughter, and you will need to do everything you can to make amends and restore fellowship there. Though you will be man and wife, living on your own, you are still tied to the Drabbles as their daughter and son-in-law, and eventually you'll have children who will be their grandchildren. You're burning a very big bridge here, and it will take time and effort to rebuild it."

"We'll deal with that later."

"Then we'll need a witness to make things legal. I'll perform the ceremony, and I'll mail the registration papers to the court-house over at the county seat first thing Monday morning." Silas pushed himself upright. "I'll go knock on Ned Meeker's door. He and his wife can stand up with you."

Having one of the elders there might deflect some of the coming Drabble wrath. But then again, it might just draw Ned into her crosshairs. Still, Ned lived closest to the church. And he could be counted on not to run straight to the Drabble house and sound the alarm.

Ned and Trudy came, roused from their bed and hastily dressed. Ned glanced at Silas's eye but asked no questions. After hearing why the pastor had knocked on their door so late, they agreed to serve as witnesses, though Trudy's brow wrinkled, and she asked Alicia twice if this was what she really wanted.

The ceremony was simple, unadorned,

and quick. His heart broke for the young couple. This couldn't have been the wedding Alicia had envisioned. They would have some rough days ahead. The path was always more complicated and full of pitfalls when things weren't done God's way. They were so in love, so desperate to be together, they'd compromised what was best about love and marriage.

It was a sobering lesson not to sacrifice the future on the altar of the immediate.

FOURTEEN

Silas arose early in spite of not getting to bed the night before until well after midnight. His reflection told him the few hours of sleep had reduced some of the swelling around his eye, but the color had come up in a purplish-blue splotch. No way to disguise or diminish the angry-looking mark.

He spent time in prayer, asking for God's wisdom to help him deal with the rift in the church. His Bible reading brought him to Proverbs four, verse eighteen.

"But the path of the just is as the shining light, that shineth more and more unto the perfect day."

"Lord, this is what I want, and what I need. Please make me a good example to my church and to those in the community who are watching. Help me to humble myself and ask for forgiveness where I need it and to extend forgiveness where it is due.

Help me to take instruction from fellow believers, but help me also to follow Your will first and foremost. Help Your light to shine through me in all my dealings with Willow, Mrs. Drabble, and the congregation. And I ask that Your will be done regarding the district supervisor's visit."

Finally feeling equipped to face the day ahead, he shrugged his way into his suit coat and tried to loosen the squirming ball of nerves in his stomach. First on the agenda, a visit to the Drabble household to begin healing the breach between them. Though he had a feeling that when he told them about Alicia and Kenneth, any hope of reconciliation would disappear.

Clouds hid the sun, and a fine spring rain pattered on the grass and made puddles on the road. Silas ducked his neck into his overcoat and hurried. Gaining the steps to the Drabble house, he shook the water from his sleeves and hat brim before knocking on the ornate oak door. Gingerbread trim dripped, and gusts of wind spattered the porch boards with droplets.

A figure moved behind the etched-glass oval in the door, and the knob rattled.

"Good morning, Hannah. I need to speak to Mr. and Mrs. Drabble. Are they home?" Silas stepped into the foyer as the young woman in the mobcap and black dress held the door.

"Good morning, Pastor Silas. It seems all I'm getting done today is answering the door. We're not used to so many early morning visitors." She smiled and shrugged, as if she realized she might've been a bit ungracious. "Please wait here. I'll go see."

When Hannah returned, she motioned for him to follow her. "They're in the breakfast room."

The smell of fried ham and hot potatoes greeted him, reminding him he'd had nothing but a slice of bread and butter — all he could force into his stomach this morning — for breakfast.

Walter Drabble looked up from his plate for an instant, grunted, and tucked back into his food. Lightning flashed, followed by a low rumble of thunder that rolled from peak to peak.

Mrs. Drabble's stare sent a tremor up Silas's spine. Her glare lingered on his black eye, and he waited for her to ask.

Instead, she creased her napkin into precise folds, laid it alongside her plate, and placed her hands in her lap. "Good morning, Reverend Hamilton. After our first visitor of the day, I thought you might come by." Her voice was so knife-edged, he wondered why she didn't choke.

A pang hit his heart. Here was his sister in Christ, a deaconess in his church, a member of his congregation, and his very presence raised her hackles to the point she could barely be civil.

"Mrs. Drabble, I've come to speak with you, to ask your forgiveness and hopefully make a start on restoring fellowship between us. It saddens me to be at odds with anyone in my church, and I hope we can get everything out into the open and come to a place of peace."

A satisfied smile stretched her lips, and she sat back in her chair. "At last." She sighed and softened, letting her shoulders and spine relax. "I knew you'd come to your senses, though I'm sorry it had to come to a head like this. I'm glad we have a chance to put all this behind us before any permanent damage was done. Please, sit down. I'm sure we can resolve everything nicely."

Silas blinked at this turnabout. He pulled out an empty chair and eased onto it, accepting the olive-branch gesture. "Mrs. Drabble, before we discuss anything else, I need to talk to you first about your daughter."

Her smile widened. "You're showing good sense at last. After everything I was told this morning, I'm not at all surprised you've come to talk about Alicia. It's only natural you'd change your mind once you had all the facts, and I assure you, I'm not one to hold a past folly against a man. I'm only sorry I sent those telegrams, but no matter now."

"Telegrams?" Mystified, Silas swallowed his apprehension and clenched his hands on his thighs.

"Yes, well, never mind. I'll take care of that later." She unfolded her napkin and motioned to Hannah. "Set a place for Reverend Hamilton. You will join us for breakfast, won't you?" Her tone took it as a matter of course. "There's so much to plan and discuss. You won't want a long engagement, will you? I think June will be best, but that only gives us about five weeks or so. Good thing I've got most of the wedding planned already."

"The wedding?"

"Yours and Alicia's, of course. That is why you came this morning, isn't it? To formalize the engagement now that you're finished with that . . . actress person?"

Silas seriously considered knocking his fist against his forehead. "Mrs. Drabble, stop. I've come to tell you that Alicia is married. She got married last night. I performed the ceremony myself."

Mr. Drabble stopped shoveling scrambled eggs into his mouth, and his wife gasped.

"That's ridiculous. Alicia is upstairs in her room asleep."

"I'm sorry, Mrs. Drabble, but she isn't. She and Kenneth Hayes came to me last night at the church, and I performed the marriage ceremony and blessed their union." Silas braced himself for the wrath to come.

Mrs. Drabble's face got redder and redder until Silas feared she might do herself harm.

"How dare you? You married them? Kenneth Hayes?" With each question her voice rose and so did her body. By the time she screeched Kenneth's name, she was on her feet leaning over the table, bracing her palms on the tablecloth.

Lightning flickered through the lace curtains, followed by a booming crash that vibrated through Silas. "Please, let me explain."

"Hannah!" Mrs. Drabble turned and shouted in the direction of the kitchen. "Go upstairs and fetch Alicia. I don't care if she's still asleep, just get her down here."

Silas gripped his knees and sought wisdom. Though he was not unused to family crises, the one looming now was by far the worst he'd dealt with. And though he'd anticipated some high emotion, he had a feeling Mrs. Drabble's response was just getting rolling.

Hannah scuttled into the room, her hands wrapped in her apron. "I'm sorry, ma'am, but she's not there. Her bed hasn't been slept in, and her personal items are missing from her dressing table." The girl's eyes rounded, and creases marred her usually serene brow.

Walter Drabble stopped munching his toast, swallowed, and shook his head. "She really did it?" He scratched the side of his head. "She threatened it, but I never thought she'd go through with it."

Mrs. Drabble subsided into her chair, her jaw open and her arms lax. The enormity of the catastrophe seemed to hit her, and she jammed her napkin to her lips, stifling a sob.

Silas swallowed. "Please, Beatrice, calm yourself. This isn't the tragedy you seem to think it is."

She stopped sobbing, and her eyes blazed. "Don't tell me to be calm. This is your fault. You should've hauled Alicia right back here the minute she showed up at the church. It was your Christian duty. If you would've done as I wanted and married her yourself, this never would've happened." This last bit came out a wail. "How am I ever going to show my face in this town again? This is all your fault. Yours and that actress. You allowed your head to be turned by a common trollop. And Alicia is the one who will pay for it."

"Mrs. Drabble, Alicia is a grown woman and capable of making up her own mind whom to marry. Kenneth and Alicia are very much in love. Though it pained Alicia to go against your wishes, she has the right of it. She needed to leave her father and mother and cleave to her husband. If I hadn't agreed to perform the ceremony, they were prepared to travel to Leadville or Idaho Springs or Denver until they found someone who would. Instead of worrying about your image and reputation in town, you should be proud your daughter chose a young man with a heart for serving God, who loves her and will spend his life trying to make her happy."

She stood trembling and glared at Silas. "If you thought to come here to resolve our differences, you have another think coming. You've helped my daughter defy me, and you'll rue the day. The whole world is going to come crashing down on you, mark my words." She stalked out of the room, her shoulders squared and her back poker straight.

Silas dragged his hand down his face, forgetting his eye and wincing when he touched it. "I'm sorry, Walter. I hate discord in the church, and I fear this situation is getting out of control. I had hoped to be able to talk things out calmly and reach some sort of an accord."

"Bea isn't one to get over things too quickly." Walter sighed and pushed his plate back. He dug in his vest pocket. "Forgot to tell you, telegram came. District supervisor will be in church tomorrow."

Willow slipped from the hotel and headed to the theater, dodging raindrops and clutching her shawl around her shoulders to ward off the chill. Too bad about the rain. She would've liked to enjoy the solace of the stream this morning, but her dressing room would have to do. Lightning played around the mountaintops, and thunder blanketed the town, drowning out even the persistent noise of the smelters and stamp mills that never ceased.

Francine's bed had been empty when Willow awoke. Odd, since Francine loved to sleep late. Still, considering their sharp words of the previous night, perhaps it was better this way. Give them both time to cool down.

Bill let her in the back door of the theater. "Morning, Miss Willow. You're not the first one here today."

"Oh? Francine came in early? I thought she'd be at breakfast still."

"Miss Francine came in a while ago, all dripping wet like she'd been out walking in the rain. Don't usually see her in such a state. But I wanted to warn you. Mr. Moncrieff's here. In his dressing room." The watchman crossed his arms. "After last night's shenanigans, you can bet I'm keeping my eye on him. If he bothers you, you just holler. I'll come running."

"Thank you, Bill." She patted his forearm. "You're a good friend."

"What he did wasn't right, and I aim to see he doesn't try it again."

"I'm sure he won't, especially not with you looking out for me."

She passed Philip's dressing room on the way to hers. A creepy feeling squirmed up her spine, and she hurried down the hall. The matinee would require all her acting abilities in full force to get through the scenes with Philip.

The deeper she went into the building, the more the rain receded. By the time she

222

got to her dressing room at the end of the hall, even the thunder failed to make much of an impression. She unwound her shawl and brushed at the raindrops on her hair and face before opening the door.

She braced herself for a confrontation with her sister, but the room was empty. And clean. Clement had kept his word and sent someone in to straighten up the disorder from last night.

Draping her shawl over the back of a chair to dry out, she moved to light a few lamps. With everything in its proper place, the only evidence of the altercation was a small crack in the corner of one of the dressing table mirrors. Francine would complain about that for sure. Willow eased down onto the chaise, putting Philip and her sister out of her mind, letting her thoughts wander to Silas and his brave defense of her. And his kisses. She touched her lips.

Engaged. It seemed so unreal to her. That she would be staying in Martin City. In her entire life she'd never lived more than six months in any location, and she'd never had a home, always living in hotels or in the theaters themselves if necessary. She didn't know how to keep house or do laundry, and as for cooking, she'd never even boiled water, much less prepared meals for a man.

Would Silas care? Perhaps the woman he currently engaged as a housekeeper would be willing to give her a few pointers. Or the Mackenzies. They'd all been so nice, especially the women. Surely Matilda, Karen, and Ellie would have good advice for her.

Footsteps sounded in the hall.

Please, pass by. Go on. Leave me alone.

The door opened, and Willow sat up.

Francine breezed in. She was halfway across the room before she seemed to notice Willow. Her footsteps slowed, and her expression hardened. "Oh, I thought you'd be with your precious Silas."

Willow sucked in a deep breath. "Francine, please, I don't want to be at odds with you."

An unladylike snort erupted from Francine, and she swung away toward the costume rack against the far wall. The clothes hangers clacked and scraped on the metal rod, and she flipped through the dresses so quickly, she couldn't possibly have examined any of them.

Willow noted Francine's wet hair and dress. "Where did you get to this morning?"

"I can't see how it's any of your concern what I do or where I go." She selected a dress and ducked behind the screen. "You're obviously going to do what you want without thinking about me anyway."

"Francine, please. I don't want to rehash everything we said last night. You're my sister and my only family. I'd like you to be happy about my coming marriage."

"Happy! I'd have been happy in New York. I spoke with Clement this morning. He told me he's sent your regrets. Regrets?" Several thumps came from behind the screen. "You're going to regret it, that I can assure you. Whatever happens is your own fault."

"My only regret in this entire situation is that you can't seem to get over the fact I've found my calling in life, and it doesn't line up with what you want." Willow rose and lifted her own costume for the first act from the rack. "And I'm sorry about that, but you throwing a fit isn't going to change my mind. I'm in love with Silas, and I'm going to marry him."

Francine emerged and propped her hands on her hips. "We'll see about that." She threw her damp dress into the corner. "I've heard his church isn't exactly happy with his choice of a bride. And if he doesn't go through with the wedding, where will you be?"

The fierceness in her eyes brought Willow up short, and uneasiness hitched up her spine. "What have you heard about his church?"

A triumphant smirk crossed Francine's features. "I know more than you think, and you'll find out soon enough." She sat down at the dressing table and turned her back. "You wouldn't listen to me, so you'll have to learn the hard way."

"Francine, please."

Her sister refused to speak, concentrating on applying her makeup.

Willow went behind the screen to change. Francine had always been moody, petulant, and more than a little selfish, but she'd never been truly vicious. Surely she was only speaking out of a place of hurt, not meaning what she said.

The clock reminded Willow they had a performance soon, and she would need to pretend not to be repulsed by Philip, not to be at odds with her sister, not to be wishing she were anywhere but in the theater. And the minute she was free, she needed to see Silas. He would make everything in her world right again. Being with him calmed her fears, assured her of his love, and made her feel like there was nothing they couldn't conquer together.

She buttoned up her costume, her fingers chilly. That was it. All her fears would be allayed if she could just see Silas. If only they didn't have two performances and a reception. And Silas would be busy with his sermon preparations. Tomorrow after church they would sort everything out.

"Is Mr. Mackenzie at home?" Silas removed his hat and stepped into the foyer of the Mackenzie home.

"Good evening, Pastor Hamilton." Buckford took his dripping coat and hat. "The family is in the parlor. I'm sure they will be glad to see you." In keeping with all Silas knew about the manservant, Buckford gave no indication he had even seen Silas's black eye, and he certainly didn't ask about it.

"Actually, I'd like to talk to Jesse privately." Though Silas loved the Mackenzie family, he needed wise counsel from one of his elders rather than an evening of fellowship.

"I see. Would you like to wait in the study while I fetch Mr. Mackenzie?" He motioned to the door on his left.

"That would be perfect. Thank you, Buckford." Silas entered the study and plucked a match from the holder on the desk to light the lamps. Red globes bathed the room in rosy-yellow light. Removing the fire screen, he poked the bed of coals glowing in the grate and added a couple of logs. Rain continued to pelt the windows.

A glance at the clock on the desk told him Willow would be in the middle of act 3 of the evening performance. With Philip. His hands fisted. Bill, the theater guard, had assured Silas that Willow would be safe, that he would watch out for her tonight. Though Silas wasn't in the habit of attending the theater on Saturdays, reserving that day for sermon preparation and prayer for the coming Sunday, it had required all his self-discipline not to show up and watch over Willow himself.

"Silas?" Jesse strode into the room, his presence as always charging the air with a feeling that nothing was impossible or as bad as it seemed. A more capable, stalwart man Silas had never known.

"Evening, Jesse. I'm sorry to drop in on you like this."

"Nonsense. You know you're always welcome. Anyway, you're being here saves me a trip. I was just heading into town to see you." He shook Silas's hand. "That's some shiner. Did you walk into a door?"

"Not exactly. I ran into a fist."

"Oh?"

As succinctly as possible, Silas recounted the events. "The eye will heal. What's important is Willow wasn't harmed, and Philip Moncrieff will think twice before he bothers her again."

"Good for you. I'm not a man of violence, but there are times when it is the most effective and reasonable response."

Silas nodded. "Why were you coming to see me?"

Jesse grimaced. "There's trouble brewing. Ned Meeker stopped by this afternoon and told me that Larry Horton and Mrs. Drabble had their heads together over at Drabble's Store, and when they saw him, they hushed up right quick, but not before he heard your name and Willow's."

Silas rubbed his hand down his face. "I've never dealt with anything like this before. It seems no matter how much I try to placate Mrs. Drabble, things just get worse and worse. That's what I wanted to talk to you about. I visited the Drabble home this morning with the unpopular news that Alicia is now married."

Jesse's eyebrows rose, and he bent to poke the fire. "Who did she marry, and how did you find out about it?"

"She married Kenneth Hayes, one of your shift foremen, and I found out about it because I was the one who performed the ceremony."

"Hmm. Kenneth came to me yesterday morning and asked for a week off to take care of a family matter. Didn't know he meant to get married. Well, that's a poke in the eye for old Beatrice, isn't it? How'd she take the news?"

"About like you'd expect. I tried to reason with her, but she's blaming me for not dragging Alicia home and running Kenneth off."

"Why didn't you?"

"I had some very good reasons for going ahead with the wedding, but I can't go into them with you. You'll have to trust me when I say their getting married was the right thing to do."

"I see."

"But I'm afraid Mrs. Drabble will never forgive me. And Alicia's marriage is only part of the reason for her antagonism. Jesse, I'm worried. Mrs. Drabble's unhappiness with me is just the sort of canker to spread right through a church. It's already divided the board, and it's only a matter of time before it divides the church."

Jesse eased onto the settee and motioned for Silas to sit in a chair opposite him. "Sadly, I'm afraid it already has. More than one person has asked me about your relationship with Willow. I've told them all I support you, and if they have a problem they should talk to you personally. I've seen this kind of thing happen before, and I'd do about anything to head it off. If it continues, pretty soon folks are deciding which side of the church aisle they'll sit on, and little things that shouldn't be a problem become a shooting war. And the major casualty is the church. Gives the congregation a black eye worse than yours."

Silas dragged his hand across the nape of his neck. "How did we get here, Jesse? All I want is to be a good pastor. I went against my father's express wishes when I took this church. I turned my back on everything he'd planned for me. And it wasn't a decision I made lightly. I prayed and prayed about coming to Martin City, and I was sure God had brought me here."

"What makes you think He didn't?"

"How can a church in turmoil be God's will? If I hadn't come here — if a married man with a family had taken the position — Mrs. Drabble wouldn't have been obsessed with Alicia marrying the minister. She wouldn't have become dead set against Willow. And the ministry here wouldn't be in jeopardy."

"What does Willow say about all of this?"

"She doesn't know. I haven't seen her today. Saturdays are extra busy for her with two performances, and I try to focus on the preparations for Sunday services. Willow knows some people have skewed ideas about actresses and such, but she doesn't know of Beatrice's animosity. I thought if the church folks just got to know Willow, they'd see what a wonderful person she is and what a great pastor's wife she would make."

"She is a wonderful person, and folks will come around if they only give her a chance."

"But will they give her that chance before the district supervisor visits and finds the church in an uproar?" Silas pulled the telegram from his pocket. "Walter Drabble gave this to me this morning. The Reverend Archibald Sash will arrive on the midnight train and be attending church tomorrow morning. The Drabbles are meeting his train and taking him home with them tonight. I can only imagine what they will say to him. After the services, there is a board meeting, followed by a one-on-one interview for me. When is the church supposed to have time to change their minds about Willow?"

Jesse grimaced, showing a fair number of teeth. "What rotten timing." He rubbed his chin. "I don't want you to take this the wrong way or assume I'm anywhere but squarely behind you on this, but is there any chance you can maybe back off things with Willow to let people get used to the idea? Just to lessen the tension and give folks time to come to their senses?"

Only the sincerity and warmth in Jesse's expression kept Silas from giving in to the despair rising in his chest. "I can't. I've asked Willow to marry me, and she's agreed. I can't back away, and I wouldn't even if I could. Giving in to Mrs. Drabble's tyranny isn't the way to heal the church. I'd only be prolonging the trouble."

"You're right. It wouldn't be fair to Willow, and it wouldn't change anything for tomorrow. It's like we're sitting on a powder keg, and there's a fuse burning."

Silas nodded, his heart sinking. "I don't know how we got here so quickly. Everything was fine, or so I thought, and within the space of a few weeks, the church is coming apart at the seams. I feel as if God is asking me to choose between my church and the woman I love. I was sure I was supposed to pastor the Martin City Church, and I was sure I was supposed to marry Willow, and now I'm not sure of anything."

"I'm not saying you're right about God wanting you to choose, but if you had to, would you walk away from this ministry to be with Willow? Or would you walk away from Willow for the Martin City Church?"

Silas tunneled his fingers through his hair. "I don't know. Right now I feel as if either would rip my heart out. How can I turn my back on my ministry, on my flock? And yet, how can I let Willow go?" He pounded his fists on his thighs. "I can't. There has to be another way."

FIFTEEN

Silas arose from a troubled sleep to a world washed new and blanketed in sunshine. It was out of balance with the sense of foreboding in his chest. The vigor that usually surged through him on a Sunday morning eluded him. As he dressed in his starched shirt and freshly pressed suit, he felt as if he were donning armor, one piece at a time.

He glanced out the window across the lawn to the church. How odd that the storm clouds had cleared from the sky yet still seemed to hang over the cupola.

Lord, I don't believe You want to force me to choose between the church and Willow, and I pray that You would go before me, that You would work in the hearts of the congregation so that a choice isn't necessary.

Sherman regarded him with solemn eyes from the bedroom doorway. That cat was like another conscience with his penetrating stares.

And Lord, if I'm misreading everything, then please open my eyes. Show me what to do, and give me the strength to do it. Make me willing to sacrifice my desires to Your will.

Unable to face the idea of breakfast, he strode across the wet grass to open up the church and prepare for the service.

Willow ignored the tea tray on the dressing table. "Francine, I want to know what you're up to. Where are you going on a Sunday morning all dressed up?"

"I can't see how that's any of your affair." The squashing reply came in an airy voice.

Willow picked up her Bible and purse. "I'm going to church. Will you be here when I get back?"

Francine shrugged and skewered her cartwheel hat to her hair with a couple of wicked-looking hatpins. "I don't know. Depends on what happens this morning."

The tickle of unease that had flitted through Willow's chest when Francine rose early that morning developed into a nubby-fingered fist prodding her innards. "What are you up to?" she asked again.

"I would think, rather than poking your nose into my affairs, you would be wise to look out for your own. Why don't you give some thought to the dismal performance you put on yesterday? I've never seen anything so hideous as you standing poker stiff in Philip's arms. You were supposed to be declaring Jane's love for Mr. Rochester, but you sounded more like you were reciting the times tables. I was so embarrassed I could hardly keep watching you from the wings." Francine rolled her eyes and touched her nose with a powder puff. "Even Clement commented on your wretched performance. It wouldn't surprise me a bit if he didn't replace you as Jane, since it's obvious you can't work with Philip any longer."

Willow's throat lurched. Yesterday had been awful, but she hadn't been able to help it. Every time Philip stepped onto the stage, her flesh crawled, and she wanted to run away.

"It isn't as if he didn't apologize to you," Francine said. "And very nicely, too, in front of the entire cast and crew. You're the one who won't forgive, for all your pious talk. And you engaged to a minister." Her thrust went deeply, as she must've known it would. A triumphant little smile played around Francine's lips, and she straightened from the mirror with a supercilious arch to her brow. "You're going to be late to church if you don't hurry."

Willow glanced at the clock, picked up her hat, and left. But Francine's accusations followed her every step of the way to the church, as did the sense of foreboding she'd awakened with.

Silas tried to quell his rioting nerves as he left the anteroom to his office and stepped into the sanctuary. He placed his Bible and notes on the pulpit and took his seat as parishioners arrived and got settled. The church organist played the prelude, and he scanned the congregation. Tension painted the air, pulling on his thoughts, stealing the peace he usually encountered before a Sunday service.

Congregants continued to file in. The Mackenzies entered, Jesse and Matilda, David and Karen with Celeste and the baby, Sam and Ellie with Phin and Tick. They came all the way to the front and filled an entire pew. Jesse wore a foreboding expression, and David and Sam only a little less so. While it warmed Silas's heart to know they were ready to fight for him, he grieved that such a stand was necessary.

Behind the Mackenzies sat a row of miners. When he met their eyes, they nodded and smiled. Ned and Mrs. Meeker sat with them.

The Drabbles arrived, and between husband and wife strode the portly figure of Reverend Archibald Sash. Mrs. Drabble's mouth wore a pinched, rhubarb smile, and Reverend Sash looked sternly out over his gray whiskers.

Proper etiquette dictated that Silas should rise and greet the district supervisor, but halfway out of his seat, he froze, staring at the doors.

Willow was as fresh and beautiful as always. She stood in the doorway, scanning the crowd.

Jesse, with an agility that belied his years, left his seat and went to Willow's side. Tucking her hand into the crook of his elbow, he led her to the front row to sit with the Mackenzies in their already-full pew.

Silas could almost see the daggers flying from the Drabble pew across the aisle. Willow, sweetly bewildered, sat between Jesse and Matilda, smoothed her skirts, and sought Silas's face. Her smile, tremulous at first then more confident, warmed him through. Just seeing her settled his nerves and made him think there was nothing they couldn't conquer together. They would get through today and have all their tomorrows waiting.

He broke eye contact with Willow, gath-

239

ered his thoughts, and remembered he was supposed to greet Reverend Sash. Halfway down the steps to the Drabble pew, he halted once more, his attention drawn by a commotion in the foyer.

Laughing, talking, and jostling, a dozen people entered the sanctuary and filed into the last rows. Francine Starr and Philip Moncrieff led the group, the first time any of the actors besides Willow had come to the church. Even from this distance, Philip's bruises stood out, much as Silas's had when he'd checked his eye in the mirror this morning.

His glance went to Willow, who had turned to look at the noise. Her mouth opened, and she gripped the back of the pew. Clearly, she hadn't known they were coming. What did they want? Clement Nielson brought up the rear, his hands shoved into his pockets and his tie askew.

Quickly entering behind the actors, Kenneth and Alicia Hayes slipped in, both beaming and self-conscious, their hands linked. They slipped into the back pew opposite Francine and company. Hardly an empty seat remained in the church.

The organist finished the song, and silence descended. Silas, suddenly aware that he stood halfway between the platform and the rail, shook his head and retreated. He'd greet Reverend Sash after the service. He couldn't take any more shocks before his sermon.

When he reached the pulpit, he forced a smile and laid his hands on the cover of his Bible already waiting there for him. "Good morning." With all the turmoil in his mind, his voice sounded far away. He cleared his throat. "I'd like to welcome you all to church this morning, especially our guests. The Reverend Archibald Sash is with us this morning, as well as several other visitors."

The back door opened, and Silas found himself staring into the eyes of the last person he'd expected — the Reverend Doctor Clyburn Hamilton.

Silas couldn't say how he got through the sermon, not with his father's eyes boring into him from the back where he'd slid into the pew alongside Kenneth and Alicia. Mrs. Drabble continued to glare at him from the front row, and Francine and Moncrieff laughed and whispered constantly. He could hardly find a safe place to rest his gaze and had to settle for staring at the back wall for much of the service. With the tension mounting in the congregation, he doubted they were listening anyway.

At last they finished the final hymn. Silas closed his hymnal, but not a soul moved toward the exit. Something was afoot, and Silas's breath shortened as Jesse Mackenzie rose and turned to address the congregation.

"Friends, it has come to my attention this morning that we have a matter to discuss as a church body. I know we have a lot of visitors, some of them quite distinguished." He nodded to Reverend Sash, who inclined his head. "If any of you visitors don't want to stay for an impromptu congregation meeting, now's the time to skedaddle."

No one moved. Silas stayed in the pulpit, not knowing what to do. Jesse hadn't told him anything about a congregational meeting. What could've occurred between last night and this morning? What must his father and Reverend Sash be thinking?

"This morning one of our board members came to my house early with an accusation against someone in this church. If these rumors are true, the person they are against must be dealt with. If they are not true, then the person who has started the rumor and those who have carried it on must be dealt with."

Silas's knees trembled. Jesse's voice commanded attention and brooked no argument. He continued. "First, Pastor Hamilton knows nothing of these rumors. I thought it best not to disturb his sermon preparations this morning by telling him something that would undoubtedly upset him and is probably not true in the first place."

Mrs. Drabble sputtered and jerked. "Not true? I have it on good authority."

"That remains to be seen, and you'll stay quiet until you're called upon." He pointed to Mr. Drabble. "Walter, keep her quiet, or you'll both wait outside."

His sharp tone set Mrs. Drabble back into her seat.

Silas cleared his throat. "I don't know what this is all about, but I'm sensing whatever it is has the potential to cause some heated debate. I would suggest we open with prayer, and then, all of us need to take it upon ourselves to remain calm and to weigh our words carefully."

"Good idea." Jesse resumed his seat.

Silas swallowed, trying to moisten his dry mouth. "Lord, we ask Your guidance on this meeting. We ask that whatever is said and done here would glorify You and unify this church rather than divide it. Amen."

Before Jesse could take over again, Silas stepped around from behind the pulpit and descended the steps to stand in the aisle. "I'm glad we're having this meeting, because there are a few things I need to address. Jesse?"

"Go right ahead."

Silas turned to his congregation, trying to ignore the runaway train feeling coursing through his body. "As you are all aware of by now, I have been courting Miss Willow Starr for the past few weeks." He flicked a glance at her pale face and lustrous eyes. "I realize some of you have a misconception about the work Miss Starr does. These misconceptions have taken hold in your minds and caused some of you to form opinions based upon lies, not facts."

Aware of both Sash and his father, Silas took a deep breath and forged on. "Miss Starr is an actress. She is a talented thespian who has studied her craft and worked hard to achieve her success. She is also a fellow believer. A sister in Christ, and a woman of high moral character. She is not, as some have claimed, a loose woman, a charlatan, or deceiver. I happen to love Willow Starr, and I've asked her to be my wife."

A ripple went through the crowd. Silas ignored them and held out his hand to Willow. She appeared dazed, but rose and edged past Jesse. When their fingers locked,

Silas's heart surged. He turned Willow to face the church and put his arm around her waist. "She has graciously consented to marry me, and I'm thrilled. She will be an excellent helpmeet for me and a wonderful addition to our church."

Mrs. Drabble jolted to her feet. "Never. Never while I live and breathe will a woman of her type live in the manse. You have been duped, Reverend Hamilton. I have it on good authority she has had more than one illicit affair in her lifetime and has, even since arriving in our fair city, been seen cavorting with a man in a cabin south of town."

SIXTEEN

Willow sucked in a breath, and black dots appeared at the edge of her vision. The thrill she'd experienced when Silas vowed his love for her before his congregation fled in the face of such a bold-faced lie.

"I never!"

"Don't lie to me or this church any longer." Mrs. Drabble's face reddened. "You should be ashamed of yourself, waltzing in here and turning our pastor's head with your flirtatious ways. You've done enough damage here, and I intend to see it goes no further. Not only are you unfit to be a pastor's wife, you've dragged him down with you. Look at his face. He's been brawling with other men over your affections."

Silas's arm tightened around Willow's waist. He gently put her behind him. "Mrs. Drabble, you're making serious accusations you had best be able to substantiate." He turned to Jesse. "Is this what you were starting to say?"

"Yes, son, it is. I'm as sorry as I can be that it spilled out like this, but maybe it's better to deal with it and get it done."

Willow edged around Silas to face her accuser. "Who told you such a thing?"

"Your own sister. Yesterday morning. Came right to my house to tell me, since you'd let her know you were going to marry our pastor. She said she couldn't rest easy unless the church knew what kind of woman you were." Mrs. Drabble crossed her arms and thrust her chin in the air. "And I guess we know now, don't we?"

The shock of betrayal went clear through Willow as if she'd been impaled. So many pieces fell into place. Francine's vow that Willow would be sorry for turning down the job in New York, her absence from the room early yesterday morning, her desire to be here today to see the destruction she had caused. Betrayal gave way to anger, which gave way to a strength-sapping sadness that her sister could be so cruel.

She searched for Francine, who set her jaw, crossed her arms, and glared back. Completely unrepentant and unashamed.

"It isn't true." The words limped out, wounded and lame. Willow's hands trembled and she gripped the end of a pew to keep her balance.

"Do you think I'm a fool? I didn't just take your sister's word for it. I went to the cabin she described, and I found this." Beatrice dug in her handbag and pulled out a handkerchief. "Are those not your initials?"

Her monogram, in palest green, screamed at her from the linen square. The handkerchief Willow had given to Alicia to mop her tears when Willow had come across Kenneth and Alicia in a cabin in the woods.

A gasp from the back of the room drew Willow's attention. Alicia had her hand over her mouth.

To say how the handkerchief came to be at the cabin would be to betray the young couple. She couldn't do that, not in front of the entire church. "Yes, that's my handkerchief."

"I knew it."

Willow turned to Silas. "I'm so sorry. I never meant for any of this to happen."

His dark eyes burned with questions, and her heart ripped in two. "It isn't true. I won't believe it."

"Silas, I can't marry you. Mrs. Drabble's right. I've done terrible damage here today." She'd come between Silas and his church, caused nothing but strife, dragged her sister's vindictive wickedness into their midst, and shamed Silas in front of his friends and a visiting reverend. Snatching the handkerchief from Mrs. Drabble's hand, Willow ran up the aisle and outside before the sobs wrenching her throat could come out.

Silas stood rooted to the spot for a moment before heading after her. Jesse's hand restrained him, and it was all Silas could do not to shove the older man away.

"Son, we need to deal with this first, and then you can deal with that." Jesse waved to Willow's retreating form.

Silas quivered, whether from shock, anger, or both, he didn't know. The force of his feelings startled him. He hadn't felt so primitive since slugging Philip Moncrieff.

Francine gathered herself to leave, and this time Silas did shake off Jesse's hand. He sprinted up the aisle and closed the doors. "Nobody leaves, especially not you, Francine."

She slunk back to her seat.

"You should be ashamed of yourself, lying like that about your own sister."

Clamping her lips shut, Francine stared back at him from under insolent lashes.

Mrs. Drabble propped her fists on her

hips. "What more proof do you need that she didn't lie? That handkerchief proves Willow was in that cabin, and you heard her yourself. She confessed."

Silas's father rose from the back pew. In all the uproar, Silas had forgotten his father's presence. "Son, I'll guard the doors. I believe your place is up front."

Though his father's eyes couldn't exactly be called kindly, there was a fair bit of staunch support gleaming there. Silas nodded and strode to the front of the church praying with every step God would give him the right words to say. And that He would watch over Willow until Silas could get to her.

"Mrs. Drabble, please take your seat." Silas leaned against the rail and crossed his arms. "As your pastor, it breaks my heart to see the manner in which this — I suppose it amounts to a disciplinary hearing — has been conducted. Rather than you, Mrs. Drabble, going to Willow to ask if these accusations were true, or even taking one or two other believers with you to ask, you've chosen a public venue, hoping to shame Willow in front of as many people as possible."

He glanced from face to face. "Do you know the purpose of church discipline? It's provided to us as a means of reconciling a brother or sister, not as a weapon to wield against those we don't like. Whatever your accusations against Willow, choosing to expose them here was wrong of you. You weren't seeking a reconciliation or restoration to fellowship. Your motives weren't nearly as pure as that. What was it? Revenge for my not marrying Alicia? Pride in the power you wield over your husband and those you tyrannize? Or just frustration that you couldn't manipulate me the way you wanted?"

Mrs. Drabble gaped and blinked.

"Whatever your motivations, it stops now. You say you have proof Willow was meeting a man in the woods? Because you have her handkerchief?" He shook his head. "Paltry proof at best. Maybe she dropped it on one of her rambles along the stream. Maybe someone else took it and put it there." He stared hard at Francine. "However it got there, I know for certain Willow didn't leave it behind after dallying with a man in that cabin."

"How do you know?" Larry Horton, who had been silent until now, stood up behind Beatrice Drabble.

"Because I know Willow. I know her character."

"That's not good enough."

Alicia rose from her place beside Kenneth. "Stop it. All of you."

"Alicia!" Beatrice choked on her daughter's name. "What are you doing here?"

"I'm stopping this terrible farce from continuing. Willow wasn't meeting a lover in that cabin."

"Alicia," Silas said, "you don't have to do this."

Kenneth stood and took her hand. "Yes, we both do. We can't let Willow be attacked like this and not try to help her." He squared his shoulders and faced the congregation and his mother-in-law. "Mrs. Drabble, it wasn't Willow. It was Alicia meeting me. Because you forbid me to court her, we met in the woods at a cabin. Willow found us there. She told us we had to come clean, but we were afraid you'd send Alicia away."

Alicia bit her lip and blinked rapidly, but she kept her chin up.

Kenneth slipped his arm around her waist. "We owe the congregation an apology, and we ask for your forgiveness. It was wrong of us to sneak off together, and we've done everything we can to make it right. Pastor Hamilton married us Friday evening."

Beatrice Drabble crumpled and covered her face with her hands. "How could you do this to me?"

Silas nodded to Kenneth, who sat, drawing Alicia down with him. Every eye in the room focused on Silas. His father stood with his shoulders against the doors and his arms crossed.

Silas took a fortifying breath. "Folks, it's plain some of you have been given some wrong information about my fiancée, Willow. I'm asking you to please get to know her before you make up your minds about what kind of a woman she is. I'm also asking you to trust my judgment in this matter. I would never court a woman I thought wouldn't be an asset to me, because God has placed His calling on my life to be a pastor. The truth is I don't know how much longer I will be your minister here." He indicated the front row. "The Reverend Sash is here to evaluate my performance as your shepherd, and I fear after today, he might feel the church would be better off with another leader."

A murmur went through the congregation, but Silas ignored it. "The truth is I'm far from perfect. I've made mistakes, but Willow isn't one of them. Oh, and while I have your attention, and because I don't want any more rumors running rampant, I should explain my black eye. I got it defending Willow from the unwanted attentions of another man." He flexed his sore fist and smiled ruefully. "Though I don't advocate violence, there are times when it is the only means available."

Philip Moncrieff shifted in his seat as several of his cast members leaned forward to gauge his reaction.

"Now, I'm going to leave you all in the capable hands of the board. Jesse and Ned and Larry and Walter will be meeting with Reverend Sash, and I imagine my father, Dr. Hamilton" — Silas indicated his father in the back — "who is in attendance today. But before I go, I want you to know I bear no malice toward anyone here. I ask that you move forward in a way that would make reconciliation possible with restoration as your goal. I ask that you accept apologies that are given and extend forgiveness to one another. And if you, as a church, or as a board, or as the denomination officers, decide this church would be better off with another pastor, I submit to that decision. But you all need to know that if you want me as your pastor, you will accept, welcome, and honor Willow as my wife."

Jesse rose and held out his hand, shaking Silas's firmly. "Go after her. We'll take care of things here, and I'll come and find you when we're done."

Silas headed out of the church. Jesse's voice followed him, excusing the visitors.

His father clapped him on the shoulder as he hurried by. "We'll talk later, son."

Not stopping, he flicked his hand to let his father know he'd heard him. He had one destination in mind, and he found her exactly where he expected.

Willow huddled on the rock by the stream, hugging her shins and resting her forehead on her knees. She'd ruined everything. In the space of a single spring, she'd started an earthquake in a church, fractured the acting company, thrown away her future — not once, but twice — and managed to disgrace the man she loved more than anything in the world in front of his congregation.

Her sister's betrayal and the accusations and rumors Mrs. Drabble had flung at Willow in front of the congregation shamed her to the core. How did one combat such lies? She had no defense that wouldn't betray Kenneth and Alicia. The rancor in the church proved she would never be accepted here, that she'd done irreparable damage to Silas.

Too distraught to cry, she could only rock,

hugging the ache to herself, sending out wordless prayers, begging God to understand what she was too wounded to say.

Footfalls dislodged pebbles on the path behind her, and she lifted her face. If only whoever it was would pass by and leave her alone.

"I knew I'd find you here."

Silas. She spun around, almost losing her balance and scrabbling to stand.

"Easy there. Seems I'm always about knocking you into the drink." He hopped down the last bit of bank and grasped her elbows.

Standing on the rock with him on the dirt, their eyes were level. "What are you doing here?"

"I came to find my fiancée. She left the church in a hurry."

"I didn't know what else to do. Between Francine and Mrs. Drabble . . . They lied, but I couldn't refute the lie without betraying someone else."

"I know they lied, sweetheart. And I'm sorry. I wish I'd known what they were up to so I could've spared you that."

Her chin dropped. "I'm the one who is sorry, Silas. And I understand, I really do. Breaking the engagement is the only logical choice. I won't make any more trouble. I promise." Her heart shattered like a cracker under a boot heel.

Silas tugged her off the rock and into his arms. He forced her head against his chest and rested his chin on her hair, squeezing her tight. "I imagine you're going to cause me all kinds of trouble, but I'll have you know I'm asking nothing more of life from this day onward."

She tried to ease back to look at his face, but he hugged her tighter. "Don't say anything until I tell you a few things."

The comfort of his embrace, the steady beat of his heart against her cheek, and the peace of the stream and forest glade wrapped around her. How she was going to miss this.

"First, I know all about Kenneth and Alicia, and now so does the entire church. They stood up in front of everyone and confessed their sin and announced their marriage. They cleared you of any suspicion."

"They're married?" She pulled back to look into his eyes, and he allowed it for a moment before tucking her head back under his chin.

"Yes. I performed the ceremony night before last and told Mrs. Drabble about it yesterday morning."

"She must've been furious with you. As angry as Francine was with me about refusing to take her to New York."

He brushed a kiss across the top of her head. "And together they concocted a story to rip us apart."

"And it worked. Silas, we have to break the engagement. Even though the lie has been exposed, the church is still fractured. I can't come between you and your church, between you and your calling." Willow edged out of his arms and stepped back.

"I'm not letting you go, Willow. Whether we stay here or go to another church is in the hands of God and the congregation, but wherever I go, you're going with me as my wife." His dark eyes had a flinty look.

"But you love this church. I don't want to be the cause of you having to leave."

"I do love these people, but if I leave, it won't be because of you. It will be because they no longer trust me to be their leader."

"They'd be foolish to let you go."

"And I'd be foolish to let you go." He gathered her close again. "And I promise, go or stay, I'll have no regrets."

Someone cleared his throat behind them, and they sprang apart. Jesse stood on the road above the creek bank. "I hate to break this up, but I figured you'd want to know the verdict." He smiled, the creases beside his mouth deepening. "It was unanimous. Every single member voted for you to stay on, and everyone is in favor of your marrying Willow as soon as possible."

Silas swooped Willow into his arms and swung her around. Joy burst over her as she clung to him. "Thank You, Lord. Thank You, Lord."

When he set her down, Jesse stood beside them. "After you left, Mrs. Drabble broke right down and cried, asking everyone to forgive her, and she seems to be willing to accept Kenneth as her son-in-law. That director fellow, Neilson, caught me outside the church and said for you, Willow, not to worry about the rest of your contract. He'll have your sister fill the lead role for the last week or two, and then they'll move on to their next engagement."

Willow nodded. It was for the best. She and Francine would both be better off apart.

"Oh," Jesse snapped his fingers. "I near forgot. You are both invited to our place for an engagement party tonight. Matilda invited the whole church, including your father."

"Your father?" Willow squeezed Silas's hand. "He's here?"

Silas shrugged. "I'm as surprised as you

are. He strolled into the church this morning just before the sermon."

"Seems Mrs. Drabble wired him," Jesse said, "when she wired Reverend Sash about you courting Willow. He hopped on a train the same day." He stepped back. "Well, I'll let you get back to what you were doing." He winked. "Don't forget. Our place at six o'clock."

Silas opened his arms, and Willow went into them like she was coming home. His kiss sent her head spinning. He eased back in increments, with small kisses and whispers. Cupping her face in his hands, he planted a kiss on her nose.

Her eyelids fluttered open, and she was grateful for his steadying hands.

His voice rumbled in his chest, sending a shiver across her skin. "I love you, Willow. You're my God-given gift, the woman I've been waiting for all my life. And you were definitely worth the wait."

ABOUT THE AUTHOR

Even though **Erica Vetsch** has set aside her career teaching history to high school students in order to homeschool her own children, her love of history hasn't faded. Erica's favorite books are historical novels and history books, and one of her greatest thrills is stumbling across some obscure historical factoid that makes her imagination leap. She's continually amazed at how God has allowed her to use her passion for history, romance, and daydreaming to craft historical romances that entertain readers and glorify Him. Whenever she's not following flights of fancy in her fictional world, Erica is the company bookkeeper for her family's lumber business, a mother of two terrific teens, wife to a man who is her total opposite and yet her soul mate, and an avid museum patron.